THE MUSIC AT LONG VERNEY

Fiction by Sylvia Townsend Warner

NOVELS

Lolly Willowes
Mr. Fortune's Maggot
The True Heart
Summer Will Show
After the Death of Don Juan
The Corner That Held Them
The Flint Anchor

SHORT STORIES

The Salutation
More Joy in Heaven
The Cat's Cradle–Book
A Garland of Straw
The Museum of Cheats
Winter in the Air
A Spirit Rises
Swans on an Autumn River
The Innocent and the Guilty
Kingdoms of Elfin

POSTHUMOUS COLLECTIONS

Scenes of Childhood
One Thing Leading to Another
Selected Stories
The Music at Long Verney

THE MUSIC AT LONG VERNEY

Twenty Stories

. . .

SYLVIA TOWNSEND WARNER

Edited, with an Afterword,

by Michael Steinman

Foreword by William Maxwell

COUNTERPOINT

WASHINGTON, D.C.

Library of Congress Cataloging-in-Publication Data
Warner, Sylvia Townsend, 1893–1978
The music at Long Verney : twenty stories / Sylvia Townsend Warner ;
edited, with an afterword, by Michael Steinman;
foreword by William Maxwell—1st ed.
p. cm.
ISBN 1-58243-112-4
1. England—Social life and customs—20th century—Fiction.
2. Antique dealers—Fiction. I. Steinman, Michael (Michael A.) II. Title.
PR6045.A812 M87 2001
823'.912—DC21
00-064460

FIRST EDITION

Book design by Mark McGarry
Set in Dante

Printed in the United States of America on acid-free paper that meets the
American National Standards Institute z39-48 Standard.

Counterpoint
P.O. Box 65793
Washington, DC 20035-5793

Counterpoint is a member of the Perseus Books Group.

Contents

Foreword

by William Maxwell

Sylvia Townsend Warner once said, "I write short stories for money," but it was quite untrue. She wrote to please herself, and because she had no choice. In a letter to a friend she wrote, "A story demanded to be written, and that is why I have not answered your letter before: a wrong-headed story, that would come blundering like a moth on my window, and stare in with small red eyes, and I the last writer in the world to manage such a subject. One should have more self-control. One should be able to say, Go away. You have come to the wrong inkstand, there is nothing for you here. But I am so weak-minded that I cannot even say, Come next week."

In another letter she remarked, "It may interest you to know that the whole of this story sprang from a house that happened to catch my eye as I was traveling from Lewes to Worthing . . . I gave it a glance, noticed that it was darkish, square, sat among its shrubs among sallow fields. That was all. A few days later, I had the whole story, all I needed to do was transfer it to a landscape that has not so many literary associations as Sussex. These impregnations are very odd. Inattention seems to be an essential element, just as it is in seeing ghosts. In the matter of seeing ghosts, I suspect that water is important too; a pond or a river nearby, a damp house, a rainy day."

During her lifetime she published seven novels, ten collections of short stories, a life of T. H. White that is a model of biographical writing, several volumes of poetry, and a translation of an early work by Marcel Proust—*Contre Sainte-Beuve*, a kind of trial run for his masterpiece.

She also wrote the libretto for a one-act opera about Shelley's drowning in the Bay of Lerici. It was set to music by the American composer Paul Nordoff but never produced.

Her posthumous books include two collections of short stories, edited by Susanna Pinney; a selection from her diaries, which are voluminous, edited by Claire Harman; and four volumes of correspondence—her love letters to and from Valentine Ackland, arranged by Sylvia during her lifetime and edited by Ms. Pinney; letters to and from David Garnett, edited by his son Richard; letters to and from me, mostly during the years I was her editor at *The New Yorker*, edited by Michael Steinman; and her general correspondence, edited by me. She published so much that she could not keep track of it all. The fiction in this present collection nobody was aware of until Mr. Steinman, working in libraries, came upon one story after another.

Sylvia Townsend Warner was born on December 6, 1893, at Harrow-on-the-Hill, where her father was a housemaster and taught history. What emerged from her infancy was a charming, preternaturally intelligent child. When she was old enough for kindergarten she disrupted the class by mimicking the teachers— meaning no offence—and her parents were asked to withdraw her. They then decided to educate her at home. Her mother taught her to read, from the Bible, and other basic subjects, and her father taught her history informally when they were on vacation in Wales or Switzerland. By the time she was ten she had read halfway through *Vanity Fair.*

Her mother had wanted a son, or, lacking that, a girl who was beautiful and had all the social graces. Sylvia was a squinty-eyed child who had to be fitted for glasses. She also inherited the family jaw. Sometimes when her mother went out for the afternoon her father brought her down to his study for tea. It was a dusky room partly below ground level, smelling of tobacco and wood shavings, with a workbench and carpenter's tools in it and a huge rocking horse that stood ten hands high. Sitting on it, with the child on his lap, he rocked and recited "La Belle Dame sans Merci hath thee in thrall..." Or she would pull books from the shelves and examine them. The thing she couldn't do was to open the green baize door that separated his study from the classrooms. Though she was probably more intelligent and gifted than any of the boys he lavished his pedagogical skills on, she had to take what was left over. He was such a brilliant teacher that even that was not negligible and may have been the reason why in her novels the reader gets such an acute sense of what it was like, for instance, to be living in France during the Revolution of 1848 or on a South Sea Island when Victoria was on the throne of England. When her mother looked up from her book to remark that she would have been better at entertaining royalty than were the people with whom Charles II took refuge after the battle of Worcester, he remarked under his breath that Charles II was easily entertained. On this slight evidence I suspect that his habitual conversational mode, like that of most schoolmasters, was sardonic. He and Sylvia were thick as thieves.

Her mother was born in southern India. In the story "My Father,

My Mother, the Bentleys, the Poodle, Lord Kitchener, and the Mouse" this paragraph occurs: "My mother's recollections of her childhood in India were so vivid to her that they became inseparably part of my own childhood, like the arabesques of a wallpaper showing through a coat of distemper. It was I who saw the baby cobras... It was to me that the man fishing in the Adyar River gave the little pink-and-yellow fish which I afterwards laid away among my mother's nightdresses, alone in a darkened room under a swaying punkah. It was I who made sweet-scented necklaces by threading horsehair through the tamarind blossoms which fell on the garden's watered lawns. I was there when the ceiling cloth broke and pink baby rats dropped on the dining-room table; when the gardener held up that dead snake at arm's stretch and still there was a length of snake dragging on the ground; when the scorpion bit the ayah. It was my bearer who led me on my pony through a tangle of narrow streets, and held me up so that I saw through a latticed window a boy child and a girl child, swathed in tinsel and embroideries and with marigold wreaths around their necks, sitting cross-legged on the ground among small dishes of sweetmeats, and who then made me promise never to tell my parents—which I never did.... It was I, wearing a wreath of artificial forget-me-nots, who drove to St. George's Cathedral to be a bridesmaid, with an earthenware jar in the carriage, from which water was continually ladled out and poured over my head; for this being an English wedding it had to take place in the worst heat of the day.... It was I whom the twirling masoola boat carried through the surf to the P. & O. liner, on the first stage of a journey towards an unknown land which was called home."

She studied the piano and musical theory with Percy Buck, the music master at Harrow. When she was nineteen she entered on a clandestine love affair with him. He was married and had five children and she had no intention of upsetting his marriage. Their affair lasted seventeen years, was never very ardent, and perhaps she did it by way of thumbing her nose at her mother. She made herself into such an erudite musicologist that she was asked to serve with a four-member committee searching out and editing sixteenth-century music, which existed often only in manuscripts to be found in the organ lofts of cathedrals. The project was funded by the Carnegie Trust. The result of their labor was the monumental ten-volume *Tudor Church Music*.

In 1916 her father died—she was convinced of a broken heart because so many of his most promising pupils were being killed in Flanders. Long after the fact, she wrote an American friend: "My father died when I was twenty-two, and I was mutilated. He was fifty-one, and we were making plans of what we would do together when he retired. It was as though I had been crippled and at the same moment realized that I must make my journey alone."

Grief made her mother impossible to live with. The three-pounds-a-week stipend paid by the Carnegie Trust made it possible for Sylvia to manage a flat in the Queen's Road, Bayswater.

She wanted to be a composer and had hoped to study with Schoenberg but the war in Europe made this impossible. The depth of her feeling for music is conveyed by this sentence about the music of the period of Haydn and Mozart: "I never leave off wondering at the music of that century—how it ran like a stream through that unmusical civilization, being talked through, disregarded, unprized or prized for the worse motives; and yet ran, clear, independent, between its banks with its own life and its own direction, with tributaries all along its course from here, there, everywhere."

She had many friends in London. Some of them she had known as schoolboys at Harrow. Chief among them was David Garnett, whose bookshop was the center of literary London. In Garnett's memoir *The Familiar Faces* there is a portrait of Sylvia as a young woman: "Sylvia is dark, lean and eager with rather frizzy hair. She wears spectacles and her face is constantly lighting up with amusement and intelligence and the desire to interrupt what I am saying and to cap it with something much wittier of her own. I sometimes speak slowly, waiting for the right word to come... She quivers with eagerness as though I were really going to say something good and then dashes in and transforms my sentence and my meaning into a brilliance I should have been the last person to have thought of."

On a walking trip in Dorset with the sculptor Stephen Tomlin she was introduced to the novelist Theodore Powys and his family. They lived in the tiny village of East Chaldon near the sea, and she was fascinated by them and became part of their circle, which included a handsome, elusive young woman who went by the name of Valentine Ackland and was a poet. According to Claire Harman, Sylvia's biographer, "Valentine" was a pen name; she was christened Mary Kathleen McCrory Ackland. Her father was a fashionable London dentist, the senior dental surgeon at St. Bartholomew's Hospital, and was awarded the C.B.E. for his work in reconstructing the smashed faces of soldiers. He was a melancholy man, dissatisfied with his life and unhappy with his family. Valentine sometimes believed that he loved her but it seems more likely that he loved only himself. When he discovered that she had had sex with a woman he turned on her violently and said that if she continued this practice she would go blind and possibly insane. The good old days. He died suddenly of cancer shortly after the end of the war. Valentine's mother was the daughter of a wealthy barrister and amusingly eccentric. Sylvia couldn't bear her.

Valentine as a child had no solid person to hang on to. On a whim she married a callow young man, found she did not like to be touched by him, and by swearing falsely that she was a virgin, got the marriage annulled. She was highly promiscuous, preferred women to men, but slept with both. She became pregnant, by whom Claire Harman could not discover, and miscarried. She was a secret drinker. She wore trousers, in a period when no other women did. As the result of a series of events so complicated that they might almost have been devised for a novel by Thomas Hardy, the two women shared a cottage in Dorset for a night. A forlorn remark by Valentine, from one darkened bedroom to another, propelled Sylvia into her arms. And was perhaps meant to.

Sylvia was in her late thirties, Valentine thirteen years younger. For the next forty years they lived together in what was to all intents and purposes a marriage. Sylvia cooked and gardened, Valentine was handy with an axe and dealt with their car. They lived in various places and then settled down permanently in a plain-faced house on a very small island in the River Frome, near the village of Maiden Newton, in Dorset. They shared this property with fishermen, swans, herons, a badger, a moorhen, turtles—all the water-loving creatures. When the water rose in flood time it did not always stop at the doorsills.

In 1937, because they thought Britain was on the verge of becoming a fascist state and they believed that the only alternative to Fascism was Communism, they joined the Party and attended demonstrations and Sylvia sometimes wrote for Party magazines. They were briefly in Spain during the Civil War. Eventually Valentine realized, and with some difficulty persuaded Sylvia, that Stalin was not the benign figure they had believed him to be.

Sylvia admired Valentine's poems, and together they published a volume of poetry, *Whether a Dove or Seagull*, in which they did not specify which poems were by Valentine and which by Sylvia. Valentine was always aware of how much greater Sylvia's talent was.

Sylvia was not distressed by Valentine's casual infidelities, but when she fell in love with a spoiled American woman who thought she might (and then again thought she might not) want to live permanently with Valentine, Sylvia suffered deeply and even made herself homeless until the crisis had passed. As she wrote a friend, "I was gray as a badger and never at any time a beauty but I was better at loving and being loved."

They drove through the Scottish highlands. They rented a house on the wild coast of Norfolk and were driven from it abruptly by abnormally high tides. They traveled in France and Italy.

People came for tea or on a visit—some ordinary people, some distinguished. Among them Benjamin Britten and Peter Pears, Dame Peggy Ashcroft, Nancy Cunard, David Garnett. Cutting the cake on his eightieth birthday, Ralph Vaughan Williams said, "In my next life I shall not be making music, I shall be being it."

Then a lump in Valentine's breast was found to be malignant and she had surgery, was pronounced free of cancer, and resumed her normal life, until once more she found herself a patient in Guy's Hospital, London.

After her death Sylvia lived on in the house, alone and permanently bereft.

Her lifelong publisher, Chatto & Windus, also published the Scott Moncrieff translation of Proust's *A la recherche du temps perdu*, which badly needed revising. They wanted Sylvia to do this with Andreas Mayor, but the Scott Moncrieff heirs balked—fortunately, because in her early eighties she had a great spurt of creative energy and wrote the stories about fairy-life collected in *Kingdoms of Elfin*.

They have an eerie authenticity that suggests firsthand knowledge, and contain some of her finest writing.

In the winter of 1978 old age finally caught up with her. Her swollen legs obliged her to take to her bed. When her secretary, Susanna Pinney, saw that the sheets were not being changed often enough, she took over. Sylvia had an Irish nurse, whom Claire Harman says she did not like, and Colin House, a young man who had been her yard boy and was devoted to her, also helped out. She died in his arms on May Day. Her funeral service was held in the little church at East Chaldon and her ashes were buried in the churchyard, in the same grave as Valentine Ackland's.

THE MUSIC AT LONG VERNEY

The Music at Long Verney

DURING the evening of the day after his twenty-first birthday their son said to them, "I might as well tell you now and get it over. I shan't go on with the place, you know. I shan't live here. England's sinking under lovely old houses with lovely old paupers creeping about in them like maggots in nutshells too large for them. Do what you like with it"—his mother arched her neck—"break the entail, let it go to old Gilfred to sit and sozzle in. Anything you please. But count me out. If you'll take my advice, you'll sell it and spend the rest of your days in comfort, for a change."

"Well, thank you for telling us," his father said mildly.

Two years later he was killed in Cyprus.

They were still at Long Verney when the news came. Oliver wrote immediately to tell Gilfred. A memorial service was held in the parish church and Gilfred traveled from Guernsey to attend it, wearing a fur-lined coat, and wept and belched through the ceremony. Age and alcoholism had given him a baroque magnificence. A very white toe protruded from his left boot. It distressed Gilfred to see how Oliver and Sibyl had aged. After dinner, to cheer them up, he told stories about the manageress of his residential hotel. "Shan't marry her, though," he confided. "Great-Grandfather Pusey settled in Dublin and married his landlady. But he was a very different fish. Had a walrus moustache and played the guitar."

Oliver shared the Pusey ancestry with Gilfred. This tie of blood designated him as the one to take up the subject of the entail; but Sibyl did it.

"Do you mean to say there was no one between young Noll and me? Not on your side, either? Poor young chap. Silly business, all this keeping the peace among dagos and getting shot at for your pains. No one between him and me? We *are* getting thin on the ground, aren't we? Not like the old days."

"So it will come to you at Oliver's death."

"Come to me? My dear good Sib, what should I do with it? Hand it on to the National Trust? No, you must get me out of it somehow. You've got a lawyer, I suppose. Ask him."

Threatened by inheritance, Gilfred became quite alert and clear-headed. His last words, as they stood waiting for his train, were an assurance that if she and Oliver got it all drawn up and sent him the forms, he'd make a point of signing them.

Gilfred signed his renunciation; the entail was cut. Long Verney was now their unqualified own. Oliver was seventy, Sibyl was sixty-eight. At intervals they agreed that they must discuss what to do about it. Discussion between them was almost impossible. They were first cousins, they had known each other from infancy; their tastes, their views, their upbringings were similar. There was no flint in their joint mechanism to spark off a discussion. They agreed that they really must, that they really ought, and left it at that. When anyone else ventured a suggestion, they instantly and as one disagreed with it. The cost of living was going up. The upkeep of Long

Verney was a drain on their income. But since Noll's death they were that much richer, and could manage. It was not as if they spent money on doctors or other such expensive tastes. They were healthy and abstemious; their chief pleasure was reading and Oliver was a life member of the London Library.

"They'll never leave till they go out in white stockings," said Jane Elphick to Lionella Crew, who replied, "I don't know that I really want them to leave. They've been there forever. It would be like seeing Long Verney without its chimneys, seeing it without its Furnivals."

Then Sibyl had the car accident. She had always been a good driver, was still a good driver; but she was unequipped for a generation of bad drivers. Dawn Conkling, daughter of a newly arrived farmer, was unequipped to encounter an antiquated Rolls-Royce appearing in majesty at the summit of a rise in a narrow lane. They met head on. Sibyl's car was so much the heavier that Miss Conkling's car got the worst of it. Sibyl cracked her knee. Miss Conkling broke her nose. Miss Conkling's injury was so much more demonstrative and her feelings so much younger that she brought action. The magistrates gave the case against her, but they could not give Sibyl back her knee. It stiffened.

While Oliver was acclimatizing his mind to the prospect of talking German at meals to an *au-pair* person, while Jane and Lionella were coming in to cook and make suggestions, Sibyl had privately made up her mind. No, not a hotel. No, certainly not a modern house in the village. The gamekeeper's cottage was empty, had long been empty, needed repairing. The gamekeeper's cottage must be repaired and they would move into it. "But the books?" said Oliver. She had thought of that; while the house was being repaired, the gamekeeper's shed, large and airy because of the stink of former ferrets caged there, could be made over into a library. Part of her, the part that wrote poetry, had always wanted to live in the gamekeeper's cottage, solitary in the North Wood. And Long Verney could be let. Indeed, they would need to let it, to pay for the alterations to the gamekeeper's cottage. No part of Oliver wanted to write poetry, though he enjoyed reading it aloud. But he was fond of trees, he always carried a few acorns in his pocket; he had pleasant recollections of stopping for a cup of tea at the cottage after shooting partridges; it stood on a gravel soil, the only bit of gravel soil on the estate; it would be healthy (old Jennings never had a touch of rheumatism about him); he and Sibyl would still be living in a place of their own; altogether it was an excellent scheme, couldn't be bettered. And how much wiser to find a tenant instead of selling the old place. Less abrupt.

A tenant was found. He was a London man who had been told to live in the country for his health's sake. He made no bones about the rent. His references were impeccable; he seemed literate. He had a wife and a son. His name was Simpson.

The swallows were gathering, the owls hooting in the first chilly nights, when Oliver and Sibyl settled into the gamekeeper's cottage, burrowing in as if for a hibernation. *The Gamekeeper's Cottage, Credon, near Dittenham, Oxon.* was on their new writing paper. Circulars addressed to Long Verney were redirected at the post office, and at first the old address stared through the new one, and as time went on grew inconspicuous, an appurtenance of envelopes. Long Verney was less than two miles away by road, and under a mile if one took the track through woods. But it lay in a hollow and even when the trees were bare could not be seen. On very still and frosty days an aigrette of smoke was visible. It was Sibyl who thought of it more frequently, because it was she who had dictated the move and so was more conscious of it. But in the main she thought of it as a stranger's house, since strangers were living in it.

"They sound quite awful," she said to Lionella Crew. "Quite awful." Her voice was tranquil.

"But haven't you seen them?" said Lionella.

"Oliver saw them. I don't suppose I ever shall. They don't go to church."

"But there they are living in your grounds—or should I say you are living in theirs? Anyhow, the same grounds. Suppose you met them out walking?"

"They never walk. They're the sort of people who have to go everywhere in a car."

Oliver added that the Simpsons were not the sort of people one would meet in a wood. "No dogs," he added, explanatorily.

No dogs had been a stipulation in the lease, because of the frailty of the gilded Regency staircase. It was said at one time, quite untruly, that rows of slippers lay in the Long Verney hall, as in a mosque.

"I expect you are glad to be tucked in among your trees," said Lionella. "What a rough night it was!"

With their move, Oliver and Sibyl suddenly became a matter for public concern. It was as if they had been brought out into the light of day and revealed as much older, thinner, dimmer, than was supposed; as if Long Verney were an attic in which they had been stored—inventoried, known to be there, hereditary objects on their quiet way to becoming two more family portraits. They were also Oliver Furnival, J.P. and Rector's Warden, Mrs. Furnival, a member of the Parish Council, the Women's Institute, the Gardeners and Beekeepers Association; but they had been all this for so long that it passed unnoticed. Their son's death had briefly illuminated them but nobody wanted to stress it. Sibyl's accident made her momentarily notorious but nobody wanted to stress it. With the move to the gamekeeper's cottage they fell into the public domain; everybody was interested in them, well-wishing and helpful. The curator of the Dittenham Museum stored family papers; the rector's son hung their curtains; Rudge the postman transported Sibyl's house plants in the Royal Mail van; when Mrs. Veale, the charwoman, refused to follow Sibyl to the new house (she had been rejected by the Simpsons, who brought servants of their own, and she looked on this as a deliberated insult), five notables of the Women's Institute offered themselves as replacements. With so much assistance abounding, it had been quite difficult to carry out the move.

The encompassing trees gave a sense of shelter, but in reality their creaking boughs and swooping shadows emphasized the change from a low-lying house to one on a rise of ground. The New Year was blown in by a series of gales. Every house has its particular orchestra. The gamekeeper's cottage was full of drummings and fifings; it acknowledged every change in the wind's quarter. But it was sturdy and tightly built, the drummings and fifings, blusterings and rumblings were companionable and somehow animating.

"It's like being in Sicily," Sibyl commented.

"Sicily?"

"Yes, Sicily. You remember how our holidays in Sicily were like being in another world. It was so different one couldn't imagine being anywhere else."

"Yes, Sibyl, I believe you're right. It's certainly very pleasant being here. Here's another bastard." In his fine sloping calligraphy Oliver wrote: *July ye 7th. Job Hazzle inf. Base.* He was transcribing the Parish Registers, a winter occupation. With this he was combining a per-

sonal research into the prevalence of bastardy, which varied inter-
estingly from decade to decade. He hoped to establish that bastards
were more frequent in the Puritan epoch. Job Hazzle had not been
baseborn in vain.

"1652? They're mounting up nicely, aren't they—poor little creature!" said Sibyl, reading over his shoulder. "I suppose he was one of
the Hassalls. You know, that fat family at Lower Duckett."

The keen-sighted gaze of their small gray eyes directed on the
parchment page was identical; identical the long straight noses, the
narrow heads. They were first cousins, they might have been twins.
It was an animal resemblance, as though they were dog and bitch out
of the same litter. They shared with those comparable animals the
expression of pedigree chasers and killers trained through centuries
in obedience—now gentle, undestroying, and of limited intelligence.

"But don't you ever see them?" asked Sally Butcher.

"I saw the man," said her host. "He was quite unbelievable. Dead
from the feet up. But a harmless old stick."

"I feel rather romantic about them," said Mrs. Simpson. "I hoped
they'd call. They belong to that date, you know."

"Mother-of-pearl cardcases, engraved cards, two from the caller's
husband, for the Mr. and the Mrs., and one from herself, stay for fifteen minutes," Sally Butcher supplied.

"Quite long enough," said Anthony Simpson.

"Why only one from her, Sally?" inquired her husband.

"Dames don't call on gents."

"Isn't Sally marvelous?" Nicky Butcher turned to Naomi
Simpson. "I swear one day she'll write a book."

They were sitting in the Long Verney hall, now converted to a lounge. Sally gazed at the Regency staircase. "'And did those feet'?" she said.

"'In ancient time,'" Nicky Butcher finished. "I don't believe there's a poem in the English language Sally can't quote."

A car drove up. In came the Holbeins, exclaiming at the amplitude of the hearth, the linen-fold paneling, the distance from London.

But Naomi was fond of Penny Holbein, who had been kind when her second boy was found to be a Mongolian and had to be put away in a very special and exclusive institution. She lingered in the bedroom, explaining her rather romantic feeling about the Furnivals, her sense of having ousted them, her suspicion that they hadn't called because they had taken offense, her silly inability to make the first move. Did Penny think she could ask them to a meal?

"Not too easy." Penny cocked an eyebrow. "In their own house, you know. What about Anthony? Did he like them?"

"No."

"Well, then—"

Anthony put on a Monteverdi record. He still hadn't found the right music for Long Verney. So far, Handel had fitted in best—but Handel fits anywhere. A great deal of Chopin must have been played in the house at one time. But what house hasn't had Chopin played in it? It ought to be something more homegrown: Arne, perhaps. Best of all, maybe, the counterpart music of the Church of England: Greene, Pelham Humfrey, Battishill. He must find records; if there were none, commission some. He liked the house well enough to intend on a longer lease, so it would be worthwhile taking a little trouble. Music and finance were his interests. He had an exquisite ear for both. Oliver and Sibyl had a gramophone too, with records of Noël Coward and Duke Ellington.

. . .

It was three months before Naomi could win Anthony's consent to an invitation to the Furnivals. It was a week before she could frame an invitation that would sound neighborly while acknowledging that she had never met them—the Long Verney daffodils afforded a link. When no answer came, her feeling that they were rather romantic intensified into a feeling that they had the poetry of the unobtainable. She would have left it there (unobtainables were what she normally expected) had she not learned from Jane Elphick that the Furnivals were at Amélie-les-Bains, where they had gone for a course of treatment for Sibyl's knee. Anthony had struck up a flirtation with Jane Elphick, so the second invitation was written with more confidence, the likelihood of Miss Elphick's company replacing daffodils. For the third man she had hopes of Basil, her creditable son. But the invitation was rejected, with the knee as a reason. "I never know from one day to another what it will let me do."

In actual fact, the knee was so much better that Sibyl was walking about much as usual. She was also writing poetry again, which the stiff knee had made impossible. She could only compose satisfactorily when curled up on her bed.

The trees were heavy with summer, pigeons cooed all day, and a continuous mild buzz of insects filled the woods with a sound of piety. None of this was new to Oliver and Sibyl, but it was gratifying because it was familiar. Wild strawberries were plentiful in the North Wood because of the dryer soil.

"Not so many nightingales as there used to be," said Oliver. "We can thank Simpson for that."

"Horrid man! But why?"

"One of those companies he's a director of makes weed killer."

"He would. And that silly woman, that wife of his, wishing I could have seen the daffodils. Who told you about the weed killer?"

"Grigson. He's got a nephew who's a chartered accountant."

Here a little and there a little they were learning something about their tenants. Anthony Simpson was hand in glove with the Labour Party. He was not a Jew, but his wife was. They bought nothing locally; they had sent away old Jules the onion man. Their son drove through the village at a hundred miles an hour, wore bracelets, had been sent down from Cambridge for peddling cannabis. They filled the house with ballet dancers, opera singers, photographers, and intellectuals. They were never at home for two weeks running.

As Oliver said, it was a matter for thankfulness, for if they had been modest and tolerable, they might sooner or later have had to be accepted as acquaintances.

The atoning merit of the Simpsons was that they were so often away. This was ascertainably true, for Rudge, being the postman, could be relied on. Oliver and Sibyl consulted Rudge as they consulted their barometer, and shaped their walks accordingly. No Simpson had ever been seen in the woods, no Simpson was likely to be seen there. Even if seen, they need not be met. They were the sort of people who could be heard a mile off. But naturally, one preferred to walk with an easy mind, assured that no Simpsons would start up from behind a beech tree or out of a holly brake. It was the sultry end of summer. The gamekeeper's cottage got rather stuffy toward evening. If one sat reading indoors with open windows, sooner of later it grew too dark to read; when one turned on the light, moths and blundering cockchafers flew in.

"Shall we go for a stroll?"

When Rudge pointed to Set Fair, they strolled more extensively, going beyond the North Wood, following the track downhill, skirting the wet patch where the spring oozed up among rushes and meadowsweet and trickled away to join the River Thames. The spring was a boundary point. Beyond it the track wound through the remnants of Great-Grannie's ambition of an arboretum: startling occurrences of Wellingtonias, thujas, cork trees and evergreen oaks, monkey puzzles, Norway spruces, and Monterey pines. Oliver could just remember her, sitting in a Bath chair with her sketchbook, and her crow of laughter when he pointed out that she had drawn the Wellingtonia too tall. After the arboretum one came to the thickets of rhododendrons, still called the American Garden, and then the track ran into the drive and one saw the house. Sibyl's knee was so much better that she could walk as far as this and back again without feeling any the worse for it. It became a favorite walk —known so long that they seemed to be walking through themselves. They had no sense of trespass. Their woods. Their house. They had no sense of trespass when they came out into the drive and saw the house lit up within; only of trespassers, when they noticed the row of cars drawn up in front of it. They had started their walk later than usual because they wanted to walk by moonlight, and at first sight Oliver took the lighted windows to be reflecting the moon. But only a few of the upper windows shone; it was the row of ground-floor windows, the seven windows of the long drawing room, which were lit up.

"They must have come back. How odd of Rudge!"

"They can't have needed all those cars to come back in. It must be one of their parties."

"Funny kind of party. There's no one there."

For the windows were uncurtained and showed that the room was empty.

As they watched, they saw the color of the illumination change.

The electric lights had been switched off. The room was illuminated by candles, glowed instead of shining, was mysterious and withdrawn.

"Come on," said Sibyl. "Since we're here, we'll see what's going on."

"A trifle undignified, perhaps?"

A poem had begun to flicker in Sibyl's mind and she wanted to make sure of it. "Come on."

They walked toward the house, made their way among the cars. The candlelight strengthened in the empty room. Apparently the Simpsons had respected its furnishings, except for adding more chairs and a grand piano. At one end, they had rigged up a low platform on which were four chairs and four music stands.

"Grigson said something about their being musical."

At that moment, people came laughing and talking into the room, sat down. Among them were several people the Furnivals knew; this, for some reason, made everything more improbable and dreamlike. A moment later, three men and a woman, three fiddlers and a cellist, came in, mounted the platform, poised their instruments, glanced at each other...

For it had dawned on Anthony Simpson that Haydn—who is always there, whom one always forgets—might be the solution. The few friends had been invited, Naomi's secretary rung up, and that evening he and Naomi had driven down from London, bringing the Maria Teresia Quartet with them.

All but one of the seven long windows had kept its original thin glass. None of them fitted very well, for in the course of time the woodwork had shrunk. Standing outside, Oliver and Sibyl could hear every note of the music. It seemed to be having a great many notes, though not saying much to the purpose with them. But the candlelit room and the listeners, all well attired and many of them

young, made a pretty sight. Music to hear, thought Sibyl, but rejected it, as being Shakespeare.

> *Music falls on listening faces*
> *As the rain on children falls,*
> *Wandering in woodland places*
> *Where...*

Calls, sprawls, appalls? The music flourished like a wren and left off.
The young man who had been sitting in the window seat, fidgeting,
twisting himself round, got up and left the room. Knows his own
mind, thought Oliver. The others sat on. The fiddlers did a little tuning, listening to their plucked strings like animals that hunt by ear.

"May I ask what you two are doing here?" The young man had
come out of the house. His voice was loud and aggressive.

Oliver's was clear and cold. "We were listening to the music."

Jane Elphick leaped to her feet, threw open the nearest window,
leaned out of it. "Basil! It's Mr. and Mrs. Furnival."

"Oh, oh, oh!" Moaning, stumbling over feet, without glancing at
Anthony, Naomi ran from the room. After a pause, Anthony got up
and followed her. Outside was Naomi, making a fool of herself,
Basil scorning Naomi, the Furnivals looking like tramps.

The musicians raised their bows, hesitated, decided to go on, for
this was the sort of thing one expects from the rich, and began the
minuet.

"I don't know what to say, I don't know how to apologize, I feel
so disgraced, so upset, so terribly upset, so inhospitable. The very
last thing in the world I wanted to happen. You see, it was all got up
at a moment's notice, at the very last moment; otherwise of course
I would have asked you—" On she went, making bad worse.

"The best thing you can do, Naomi," said her husband, "is to ask Mr. and Mrs. Furnival to come in for the rest of the quartet. Haydn. Your house is acoustically perfect, Furnival. Basil! Go to bed."

"Oh, will you, will you? Oh, please do! And please may I offer you something to warm you? Some vodka? A little soup? You must have got so cold, standing here."

There was nothing for it. With the poor woman in such a state and saddled with a husband who said "acoustically," they must be civil and go in. They went in, rejected the soup, drank the vodka. With all this going on, the Maria Teresia Quartet broke the minuet after its trio section and sat looking at the music before them.

"It's painful, isn't it, hanging about in the dominant," Anthony remarked to Jane Elphick.

"Oh, do you think so?"

The musicians thought so and finished the minuet. There was some tentative applause, swelled by social agony into a brisk patter.

The players began the slow movement.

The Furnivals had been put side by side on a sofa. Cushions were offered them but were repudiated. They sat bolt upright in listening attitudes. Their long thin red hands were relaxed. Their long thin legs, too long for the height of the sofa, were sharply bent at the knee. Their shoes were muddy. Each wore a whitey-brown raincoat, identical except for the sexual differentiation of buttons. Sibyl had a handkerchief knotted under her chin; Oliver held an old tweed hat dangling between his knees. It had a few fishing flies stuck in the band.

Their feet, thought Naomi, their poor wet feet. They'll catch cold. They'll die. She could not take her compassionate gaze off them. They were aware of it, but gave no sign that they were aware. If only she could put them to bed, run hot baths for them, pour in bath essence, warm her largest towels for them—they would need large towels, they were both so very tall. But it was impossible. They sat in their own house, listening to music, waiting for the music to end, identically dignified, impassive, and ridiculous. One can only hope they are enjoying the candles, thought Jane Elphick. They were church candles, made of beeswax, slow-burning, sweet-smelling, beyond the purse of any but the richest altar—and these Simpsons burned them like so many rushlights.

The slow movement farewelled itself. Oliver flicked a glance at Sibyl. The players attacked the allegro vivace. They're overdoing it, thought Anthony. His evening had been ruined; the joy with which he had listened to the first movement was irreparably past recall. What am I to say, what am I to say? thought Naomi, swept on in the allegro vivace as if in a millrace. And that—And that—Is that! It was finished.

Yes, this time it was really over. The company applauded, the players rose and bowed, everyone began to talk. The Furnivals got up. Sibyl turned to Naomi. "Thank you so much. It was delightful. Now we must be going."

It was the thing Naomi should have thought of and didn't think of. Anthony, however, had thought of it. "You must let me drive you back," he said—a trifle hastily, but he did not want Naomi flustering in. They demurred, then agreed. Anything rather than have a fuss.

Back in the gamekeeper's cottage they revived the fire with some fir cones, looked at the clock, were surprised that it was not later. The music had seemed as if it would go on forever. But the room looked lovely by candlelight.

"On the whole, Oliver, I'm quite glad we went. The music was far above my head and I never liked vodka, but I enjoyed our walk and the room looked lovely."

"It didn't seem so cold as it used to, either. And we can't blame Rudge. If they took it into their heads to come back at a moment's notice, how was he to know? Loathsome boy, though. Their son, I suppose. I ought to have knocked him down."

"It's a reason for not seeing them again."

"True, Sibyl, true. How right you always are."

Immune from any consideration of awkwardness, innocent of harm, impermeably self-righteous, they went upstairs to bed.

The Inside-Out

It was a lightless afternoon in February, not cold but with a stale cold in the air. The removal van stood outside Ullapool. Furniture was being unloaded and carried in. It was furniture the two children had known all their lives, but it looked quite different out-of-doors: gaunt, and sorry for itself. It was abashing to find that the backs of familiar wardrobes and chests of drawers were just unpainted deal. Ullapool was built of grayish brick; it was a semidetached house and the other half of it was called Sorrento. Each half had a small garage attached to it. Other grayish brick houses of the same height extended on either side. All but one had garages. That one had a gravel path and a side gate of wood trellis, and behind the gate was a holly.

A strong smell of straw, sweat, and burlap came from the van. It was an interesting smell, and Clive and Stella snuffed it as they stood on the pavement, keeping out of the way. Inside the house Mother was running to and fro, telling the removal men where to put things; Father followed her silently, as if he might be found useful; from time to time he made a suggestion and Mother's voice became patient as she explained why it wouldn't do. So they had taken themselves off to the pavement, and watched the furniture being carried into Ullapool—more and more of it; and, after the furniture, crates, some nailed down, others without lids, holding things like frying pans and baking dishes swaddled in crumpled newspaper. And their feet began to grow cold, and the smell from the van made them thirsty, and they thought poorly of Ullapool, though when they arrived and ran about its emptiness they had rather liked it.

"I think it's a beastly house," said Stella—so loudly and clearly that one of the removal men said she would feel quite different when they were properly in and the beds made up, Missie. He was a local man and felt a concern for these strangers coming into the house where the mad old lady had ended her solitary days. He went on with a crate that was so heavy it made him grunt, and was halfway upstairs with it when Mother called out, "Kitchen, man, kitchen!"

It was then she noticed them standing on the pavement, and said something to Father, who came out and said, "Why don't you explore the garden? It's got a summerhouse. The back door's open."

In the garden it seemed much nearer nightfall. It was choked with weeds and grasses of last summer, full of straggling thickets of privet and laurel, overhung by conifers. Everything was matted, entangled, overgrown, and intensely still. Some plumes of pampas grass wagged slowly in the light breeze. They seemed to be the only living thing there. As though it were part of its territory, the garden enclosed a different texture of sound: the thump of distant machinery, soft snortings of ejected steam, the clank of a freight train, whistles, the drifting cry of hooters from river tugs—noises that had been screened from the children by passing traffic when they were in the street. When they turned back and looked at the house, it already seemed quite a long way off. A light went on in an upper window.

"I don't think it's such a particularly beastly house," said Clive.

"It's pretty beastly."

He went ahead, partly because he was the elder and in double figures, partly because he was enjoying himself. It was the first time they had been in a garden other than the public garden at Worple. When Mother said, "Now that your father has been moved to the bank at Burheaton, we'll have a house with a garden," they had imagined a bowling green, swings, a Jubilee Clock, lawns, and a motor mower, just as when they were babies, at the mention of their father's bank, they imagined him rolling down it.

The garden seemed endless; endless and directionless, because at every tenth step he had to turn aside to skirt a bush, to avoid a bramble patch. Stooping under a branch, he almost fell into a bath-tub. Its white paint had mostly scaled off; what remained had a fish-belly shine. It had sifted up and was half full of a soup of dead leaves. They stirred the soup with their fingers, and tried vainly to turn the rusty taps.

"Hush, Clive! I believe I heard something. Don't breathe so hard. I believe it's hens."

"Wild hens, like in India," he said.

"Oh, goody goody!"

But hearing the noise again and listening more attentively, it seemed to him that the hens were in Sorrento.

Dense laurel hedges secluded them from the gardens on either side. A slimy network of bindweed hung on the Sorrento hedge like lace curtains, and strands of barbed wire ran inside it. Spiked iron railings backed the other hedge. Considering his reaction to this, Clive summed it up as an inside-out feeling. You couldn't get out; nobody could get in; and you wore the feeling not quite sure whether you liked it or didn't like it. Inside-out. It depended which way you put it on. He turned to consult Stella—she was sometimes quite intelligent —and she wasn't there. The inside-out feeling tightened on him. But she was close by, hidden behind a bush. With an entranced countenance she was pulling strands of ivy off the trunk of a yew tree. "Come and pull, Clivey! It's a wonderful feeling." He pulled for a little, and it was a wonderful feeling; but the smell of ivy was oppressive.

"All those little feet holding on ... There!" Another length of ivy fell on the ground.

"Oh, come on, Stella! We'll never get it all off, and it's everywhere. Come on and explore for something else."

Glancing back at the yew, she saw that the bark they had stripped was a dull red, like a graze.

"I hope we haven't hurt it. Miss Harper, who took us in Botany last term, said ivy kills trees."

Clive agreed that it had rather a killing smell.

The endless garden ended in a brick wall, too high to be seen over. Beyond it, puffs of white smoke rose into the untrammeled sky, keeping time with the soft snortings.

"But we haven't found the summerhouse," said Stella. "We must find the summerhouse."

"It's there. At least, it *was* there."

An iron frame projected from the wall. A cloak of sedge lay below. When they tried to pick it up, it fell to pieces in their hands.

They did not dwell on the disappointment; by now they were wholly in love with their garden. "We haven't seen half of it yet," said Stella. "I'm sure I saw some flowerpots near the bathtub. We could plant roses in them and make a bower round it. And grow water lilies in the bathtub like the water garden at Worple."

"I know something else, too," said Clive. "There was a scraggy place in the hedge, just after the bath. We could have a squint at Sorrento through it."

Lights had gone on in most of the houses, and curtains been drawn. "Everyone's having tea," mused Stella. "I wonder if the Burheaton baker has barley scones, like at home."

Clive said firmly he didn't suppose so. For the bathtub glimmered before them, and the scraggy place in the hedge was at hand.

"Don't tear your clothes, for goodness' sake. Remember, it's your good suit."

He squirmed into the laurels. The barbed wire had been pulled aside. He got his head and shoulders through.

"Stap my vitals!" The school had done *Scenes from Sheridan* last term, and this phrase had caught his fancy.

"Stap my vitals! They must *live* on them. Stella, come and look."

The whole of Sorrento's garden could be seen at a glance. At the near corner was a wire-netting enclosure, very neat, with some saddened hens in it. At the farther corner was a glittering glass house. The garden hadn't a weed in it, hadn't a tree in it, hadn't an inequality. And across it ran rows and rows of Brussels sprouts, exactly aligned, all of the same height, orderly as a regiment on the parade ground.

"I call it perfectly revolting," said Stella, and broke into laughter.

They squirmed back, and stood upright in their own garden, and its comfortable dusk closed round them. But now there was a compacter darkness overhead. Looking up, they saw a boy lying along the bough of a tree that rose out of the hedge. He looked as reposefully dangerous as a panther, and as watchful. He was some years older than they. His expression had a maturity of balefulness.

"Hullo," said Clive.

The boy said nothing.

"Hullo," said Clive again, and Stella said, "Good evening." Still the boy said nothing.

Ostentatiously addressing his sister, Clive remarked, "Spying."

"Trespassing," she replied; and because she was the more frightened of the two, she added scathingly, "Sorrento!"

The boy gathered himself together as if he were going to leap on them. It was his voice that leaped. "I loathe you!"

They walked away, careful not to hurry, trying not to stumble over the brambles. A voice from Ullapool cried "Tea" on a falling third. They ran. A door closed.

The boy stared down into the lost paradise, the succoring shelter from which he was driven out. The bough began to quiver with the vehemence of his dry sobbing. Tomorrow he would buy a slingshot.

Flora

A FOOTPATH branched off the track across the heath and vanished like a wild animal among the bushes. One would not have supposed it led to a dwelling—one might not have noticed it at all, if one's attention had not been arrested by a white plastic garbage bin. This assertion of civilization made the surrounding landscape more emphatically waste and solitary. But the footpath, twisting past thorn brakes and skirting boggy hollows, led to a house—the residence of Hugo Tilbury, D.Litt., F.R.S.L., named by him Ortygia. Edward, who knew the way, walked ahead. It seemed a never-ending way; I had plenty of time to muse on the donnish associations of the name and why it carried overtones of retirement, but it was too late to ask. Edward disliked conversation on country walks, alleging that one cultivated voice would scare every bird, beast, and butterfly within hearing.

He came to a pause under a group of tattered conifers and said, "There it is." Before us was a neat red brick cottage with a single chimney and a water butt. In front of it was a plot of dug ground, with some cabbages growing unwillingly in the peaty soil, fenced

with wire netting against rabbits. The cottage looked unwilling, too
—as if, being so up to date and rectangular, it felt demeaned by its
situation and wanted neighbors.

Ortygia's door was open. Edward knocked on it, and a reedy voice
said, "Come in." We entered a room containing a bicycle, some gardening tools, several pairs of gum boots, a pile of neatly folded sacks,
two pictures standing face to the wall, a narrow, painted wardrobe
with a mirrored door, and a fish kettle. Everything was clean and
orderly, as though it had been made ready for an auction. From this
strange anteroom we went into a sitting room, where Mr. Tilbury
rose from a wooden armchair and said, "Ah, Edward!" He was a
short, sturdy old man with bushy eyebrows and a trimmed beard.
Turning a bright, unseeing glance on me, he took my hand in a firm
grip and remarked that Edward had brought me, and that I was Flora
—or was I Dora? He hoped the walk had not tired me. I praised the
surrounding expanse of heath. "A protective custody," he said.

Motioning me to an armless wooden chair, he began to talk to
Edward. They talked. I sat. Their talk had the embowering intimacy
of two experts, so I felt free to study the room. It was clean and bare
as an empty snail shell—Mr. Tilbury's shell. There was a fireplace
filled with fir cones. Each of the walls had a door. As two of the
doors were above floor level, I supposed they were cupboard doors.
A highly polished sham-antique oak table was planted on a central
mat, brushed and threadbare. A fairground vase, assertively pink,
stood on the windowsill with some heather in it.

I was sufficiently tired by my walk to feel chilled, and, from feeling chilled, to feel intimidated. To rouse my spirits, I began to nurse
rebellious thoughts. Mr. Tilbury, so perfectionist in clean, bare surfaces, probably ate his dinner off the floor—if he ever dined. There
was no whiff of nourishment in the air, and the chimney pot, as I

now recalled, had no smoke coming from it. Perhaps he was an exquisite epicure, and behind those cupboard doors kept caviar, foie gras, artichoke hearts, ranks of potted delicacies from Fortnum & Mason. This was too much to suppose: I decided that what he kept in his cupboards was skeletons—skeletons on strings; that when we had gone away he would fetch them out and make them dance to their Daddy, their heels clattering on his bare boards, and that before he put them away he would polish their sallow bones.

Meanwhile he and Edward were talking about calligraphy with never a sensual thought in their minds. Taking a sharp pencil and a piece of scribbling paper from his pocket, Mr. Tilbury drew the terminating twiddle by which one could infallibly distinguish between the work of a French and a Burgundian scribe, and when Edward said yes, he saw, Mr. Tilbury put the pencil and paper back in his pocket. It was then I noticed that there was no wastepaper basket in the room.

Yet a wastepaper basket, however much Mr. Tilbury might dislike its disorderliness, would seem an essential adjunct to calligraphy. Professional scribes (French, Burgundian, what you will) must sometimes have spoiled a copy—duplicated a word, misplaced a twiddle. With parchment, this was easily put right: they scraped off the error with a sharp penknife. But when progress drove them onto paper, they must have wanted to discard a faulty page—crumple it and throw it away. Into what, if not a wastepaper basket? When did that essential adjunct to calligraphy come into use? I ransacked my memory for works of art recording it: St. Jerome in his study—in his numerous studies—Petrarch sonneteering, usurers calculating...Nowhere a trace of the wastepaper basket, not even among the Pre-Raphaelites. I forgot my place and broke into the conversation. "When was the wastepaper basket invented?"

Edward emerged from calligraphy, laughed, and said, "God knows."

Mr. Tilbury, too godlike for such an admission, impaled me on a glare and said, "That would take too long to answer, young lady."

I realized that I had foxed them both.

Some time later—it seemed like hours—Mr. Tilbury opened one of his cupboards and took out three pony glasses and a bottle labeled "Ketchup." Ketchup contained a homemade sloe gin. He filled the three glasses with a steady hand, impartially. We drank the stirrup cup and took our leave.

When we had gone a little way, Edward asked what I had made of old Hugo. I praised his sloe gin, adding that it was magnanimous of him to give me a fair share of it, since it was plain he disliked women, more especially young women who went about with young men as though they were married to them but weren't. He disliked anything he couldn't be sure of, Edward explained. The Hunter's Moon, which follows on the Harvest Moon, had risen, blackening and brightening the path. I could not believe it was the path we had come by earlier. Nothing was the same, till we came to the garbage bin, implacably itself even by moonlight. On the track across the heath, where we could walk side by side, it was as though we were freed from a constraint to remember the afternoon's visit. We planned how we could contrive a spring holiday in Portugal. Edward hoped that Mrs. Hooper of the Fox Inn would give us something hot for supper.

Yet that night he reverted to Mr. Tilbury, speculating about why he had secreted himself and his learning in that comfortless Ortygia. Some shock, some personal disaster, some scandal must have driven him there, for in conversation old Hugo revealed a livelier past, when he was sociable, knew all sorts of people, went to the opera, supped at the Café Royal (still fashionable in those days), had a top hat. It couldn't have been a religious bolt; Hugo had no more piety than a ferret. It couldn't have been money: Hugo didn't mind what he spent on something he wanted; he was poorly off for wants but not for means. And when it came to his private fortune of scholarship, he had some of the usual expert's niggardliness; from the day Edward, following the clue of a savage retort to an ass showing off in a learned periodical, had tracked him to his den on the heath, Hugo had been a most generous teacher.

Exhausted with so much exercise and open air, I kept falling asleep and reawakening with a sense of guilt that I should have taken such a dislike to the old man who had given Edward so much pleasure. In one of my wakenings I heard Edward say, "I could never repay him for all he has done for me—even if I could bring myself to give him my Kepler letter." He gave a deep sigh. The letter by Johannes Kepler was his dearest possession. He had found it in a Birmingham auction room, in a folder labeled "Letters Various and Curious." Mr. Tilbury had approved and authenticated it, and though no such vulgar phrase as "stroke of luck" had been spoken, Edward felt himself considerably advanced in his mentor's esteem. I was going to suggest he might tell Mr. Tilbury that he meant to leave it to him in his will when the sigh was followed by a contented yawn. Edward was asleep.

Five months later Edward was killed in a car crash. He died intestate. Had I told his mother that he would have wished the Kepler letter to go to Mr. Tilbury, my word would have counted for nothing, so I waited for the hour of his funeral, let myself into his flat, and stole it. It was not so easy to part with it. Not that I needed anything to remember him by, but his hand had warmed it, he had made the parchment case that held it. Eventually I brought myself to write to Mr. Tilbury, telling him of Edward's death, that he had meant to give him the Kepler letter as a token of gratitude, and that I would prefer to bring it rather than risk it in the post. The reply was brief and businesslike: he was sorry to hear of Edward's death, and would expect me on March the 10th, at 4 P.M. I took a taxi from the local station to the Fox Inn, where Mrs. Hooper exclaimed and sympathized, and gave me a drink out of hours against the cold, saying that the wind on the heath would perish a Londoner.

It was an east wind, shrill and searching—a spring-cleaning wind, I thought. From time to time, it tore rents in the cloud cover; shadows hurried over me, a distant stretch of grass suddenly became a brilliant, watery green. As I turned into the path, I looked at my watch. It was quarter to four. Everything was going to plan. The path that had been so much changed by moonlight was as much changed by bursts of sunlight; leafless thorn brakes were silver-plated with lichen, bramble patches had a smoldering richness of purple and russet.

The door of Ortygia was closed. There was a push button on it. I pressed the button, and a bell—the kind of bell that works by battery —responded with a loud jarring sound, so instantly I flinched, as if it had spat in my face. No one came. I waited and rang again, and again, for a third time, and a fourth. The door faced east, and the spring-cleaning wind pinned me to it; when I gave it a push, I found it was barred. It was the tenth of March, I had arrived at the hour Mr. Tilbury had appointed, and I did not recollect that he was deaf. If not deaf, perhaps he was dead? If so, he must be newly dead, for his patch of ground was freshly weeded; some plucked-up nettles blown against the wire fence were barely wilted. He had weeded, gone indoors, secured his door against the wind, opened a cupboard for a drink of sloe gin, had a heart attack, fallen dead, or palsied with one eye closed in a ghastly wink. That would be very awkward. I looked in through the sitting-room window. The heather had been removed from the fairground vase, and a fire of fir cones and neat billets of wood burned in the grate. Otherwise, the room was exactly as I remembered, except that Mr. Tilbury was not in it. He was not in the water butt, either—a frantic supposition, but now my imagination was keeping my courage up—for he could not have bolted the door behind him before going out to drown himself, and in any case he was not the sort of man to act without due consideration. So I went back to the door, rang the bell again, knocked, whistled, shouted his name, felt increasingly silly, wondered if I would go away—and waited on.

At twenty to five I decided I would wait till five, return to the Fox Inn, and from there ring up the police. Mr. Tilbury, I would say, had asked me to be at his house at four o'clock without fail, as I had a valuable parcel to hand over. He did not seem to be there. I was afraid something had happened to him. Etc. A flicker of amusement warmed me at the thought of loosing the police on Mr. Tilbury, who, if he retained any consciousness—perhaps he was just drunk, lying comatose with a ketchup bottle beside him—would resent this incursion on his private life. If dead, there would be headlines in the local papers—MYSTERIOUS DEATH OF WOODMELL HEATH HERMIT — and later a respectful obituary in the *Times*. If drunk, local merriment. Either way, he would give pleasure.

Meanwhile, I had my errand to attend to. I was about to make a last attempt on the bell when I heard a sound of life overhead: a loud, irrepressible sneeze, and another, and another—the sneezes of a man in perfect health but with imperfect control of his nose. I laid the Kepler letter on the doorstep and walked away.

A moment later I heard the door open. There was no need to look back; my mind's eye saw Mr. Tilbury, D.Litt., F.R.S.L., dart out, seize on his prey, and carry it into his den.

I told myself as I hurried up the path that it was the insult to Edward that made me weep tears of rage. But it was also the insult to myself. Edward was unscathed, safe dead, with his illusions intact, with his intention carried out, with nothing to revenge. I had been summoned, slighted, left to kick my heels in the cold, while Mr. Tilbury sat warming his malevolence; and no possible revenge was in my power. Attaining the garbage bin, I gave it a kick. It answered back with a multitudinous light rattle. I took off the lid. Inside was an accumulation of emptied tins that had contained a brand of ready-made rice pudding known as Lotus. The tins were spotlessly clean, as if a rat had licked them—a sturdy rat with a trim beard, a rat who in better days had supped at the Café Royal, a rat who for some reason, some personal disaster, some hounding scandal, had fled to a hiding place on the heath. Looking round on the darkening landscape, I remembered his words: "A protective custody." Even so, I could feel no pity for him.

Maternal Devotion

"I WAS TAUGHT how to make tea by Professor Abernethy in Dresden. He always used an eggcup. Not that his name was Abernethy, or anything like it," Mrs. Finch said to the young man who had come to call on her daughter. "It was more like Euston or Thompson."

As kittens bring in the mice that are too much for them to be finished off by the cat, Cordelia Finch had a habit of depositing any inconvenient suitors with her mother and leaving the rest to nature. When the Finches moved from London to Kent and their new neighbors hastened to call on them, the number of deposited suitors rose sharply. This one was a Mr. Weatherby, who was locally expected to become a Member of Parliament when he had matured. Mrs. Finch had told him that Cordelia was not at home, adding, with equal mendacity, that she hoped he would stay and have tea.

"I can't think why I should so persistently call him Abernethy," she continued. "He wasn't in the least like a biscuit."

"Some association of ideas, perhaps," Mr. Weatherby suggested.

"I don't see how it can be, for I detest Abernethy biscuits, and he was such a kind old man. He used to be followed about by a cab."

After a slight pause, Mr. Weatherby said, "Really?"

"His wife had an idea that his legs might give way suddenly," Mrs. Finch said. "He was well over ninety. Do you come of a long-lived family, Mr. Weatherby?"

Mr. Weatherby said guardedly that he had had an aunt.

"Do tell me about her," said Mrs. Finch warmly.

"There isn't much to tell, really. She lived to be eighty and died of a stroke."

"What would you like to die of?" Mrs. Finch asked. "I think, myself, there's a great deal to be said for a general atrophy, for if one has to be a nuisance, it's better not to be an active nuisance. Or would you prefer a sudden death? You might fall off a horse and be carried home dead on a five-barred gate. Do have some more cake."

"Thank you," said Mr. Weatherby. "Why a five-barred gate?"

"It's usually the gate that's nearest, I believe. 'Do the thing that's nearest, Though 'tis dull at whiles,' you know. 'Helping when you meet them—' That always seems to me such an extravagant piece of advice. Why should one help mad dogs over stiles? Why shouldn't they be able to run through underneath, as dogs in their senses do? I don't believe that even a mad dog would lose touch with reality to that extent. Or do you suppose that it really applies to idiot dogs who have lost the use of their legs, unlike Professor Abernethy? Scansion makes poets very servile. Though with a little ingenuity, and if you don't scorn classical diction, why not 'Helping when you meet them Idiot dogs o'er stiles'?"

"I should think it would be rather a waste of time. Besides"—Mr. Weatherby's eye gleamed with the acumen of debate—"how could one help dogs if one didn't meet them?"

"Exactly! Or if there wasn't a stile? Must you drag the poor creature along till you find one? I'm so glad you agree with me about poetry not interfering with one's behavior. Poets should never give good advice unless it's of the most placid description, like not turning aside to view the braes of Yarrow, or '*Prends l'éloquence et tords-lui le cou.*' I suppose chairmen at political meetings never read Verlaine."

Mr. Weatherby looked up as one who sees a momentary lighthouse through the storm. Mrs. Finch smiled at him and swept on. "If I were a poet, I would keep myself entirely to sonnets and advise no one. There are still a great many subjects without sonnets. Have you ever considered writing a sonnet sequence on the nonconforming churches? 'Stern Muggleton,' one of them might begin. And then you could have 'Equestrian Wesley' and 'Leave thou the babe unsprinkled till the work of grace has something-or-othered.'"

"Well, to tell you the worst, you know," Mr. Weatherby said, "I don't read much poetry. I don't seem to be that sort of man."

"I expect you are influenced by it, all the same," Mrs. Finch said. "Everyone is. Do you know that during Wordsworth's lifetime the population of England more than trebled itself?"

Mr. Weatherby said that he supposed Wordsworth lived a long time.

"He died," said Mrs. Finch, "at exactly the same age as your aunt."

There was a pause. Mrs. Finch broke it. "In Russia, when there is one of these awkward silences, people account for it by saying that a fool has been born."

There was another pause. Mr. Weatherby broke it. "Will your daughter hunt?" (Mr. Weatherby, who had recently put on weight, had a horse to dispose of.)

"I assure you, Mr. Weatherby, any hunting in this family will be done by me. I spend my life hunting. At this moment, I am hunting for—" Mrs. Finch broke off and rummaged among the sofa cushions. "I had the list but I seem to have mislaid it," she said. "But I remember it began with a black bishop—do you play chess?—and Mr. Harley's hat. Do you know Mr. Harley? He tunes pianos. Such a nice, somber man. If you met him in a pink dressing gown, you wouldn't know him from an El Greco, and it was so unfortunate that he lost his hat somewhere about the place. And then there was my husband's briefcase. It had a corkscrew in it and some other things. And the last thing on the list was the fire extinguisher. It's one of those clever chemical ones—you give them a smart blow and they burst into spray. Are you afraid of fire? Fire breaking out in a lunatic asylum is one of my terrors. I wonder if you are sitting on it. No, no, please don't trouble. It will be none the worse, and anyhow by the time I find it, it will be out of date. Do think this tea was made with boiling water? I don't."

Looking wistfully toward the window, Mr. Weatherby said, "I suppose you garden quite a lot."

"I've got a little watering pot. But whenever I find time to use it, it's always raining. Are you good at gardening?"

"Well, no," Mr. Weatherby said. "I spud up daisies sometimes. But my mother's frightfully keen on gardening. So was my old aunt. She gardened right up to the end."

Mrs. Finch nodded sympathetically. "I'm always alarmed when I see people plunge into gardening. Still, if your mother enjoys it . . . Besides, there is the Fifth Commandment. I read right through the Ten Commandments the other day, and I was surprised to find how many of them I agreed with. But it would have saved a lot of talk, as well as being much lighter to carry, if Moses had just boiled

36

them down to one compact little commandment—'Thou shalt not interfere.' I knew a Mrs. Prothero who was perfectly devoted to gardening, and one day when she was being shown around a friend's garden she saw a weed and tried to pull it up. It happened to be a tight-rooted wolfsbane, and while she was tussling with it, something snapped and she went blind in one eye. Could you have a plainer warning against meddling?"

While Mrs. Finch was relating this story, noises, strongly suggestive of the dangers of meddling, had broken out in the front hall—a crash, an urgent sizzling, angry words, and hurried footsteps. These were now followed by a steady swishing sound, apparently proceeding from the neighborhood of the doorstep.

"I say—" said Mr. Weatherby. Mrs. Finch looked at him devoutly, as though the lightest word from him meant more to her than any of the noises, indoors and out.

"I say!" he repeated. From where he sat, Mr. Weatherby could see a jet of high-pressured spray sweeping across the lawn.

The noises died away. A strong chemical smell remained, and grew stronger.

"I always feel so sorry for Angelo Domodossola," Mrs. Finch said. She had given up waiting for Mr. Weatherby's communication. "He, of course, was born blind, so he got about quite easily. One day, he went to see a friend. He walked right in and called, and as there was no answer, he sat down to wait. It was midwinter, and that bitter Neapolitan cold—you know how it gets into one's bones. At last, he decided to wait no longer. He put down his hand to grope for his hat and gloves and felt something clammy. It was a pool of blood. The friend had been there all the time. He had cut his throat half an hour or so before. I've never felt easy going to call on anyone since, for it is absurd to say that these coincidences never happen twice, and though I am not blind, I am very inattentive. I am sure I could sit in a room with a corpse for hours before I noticed anything was wrong."

Mr. Weatherby saw that where the spray had fallen, the grass was turning yellow.

"I suppose if one were really observant," Mrs. Finch said, "one would constantly notice that something or other was a little wrong."

"'Where ignorance'—" Mr. Weatherby began.

The door opened and a voice said, "Of all the damned, confounded places to put the damned thing in! Elinor!" Mr. Weatherby rose to his feet as Mr. Finch burst into the room.

"Sit down, sit down, Mr. Weatherby," Mrs. Finch commanded. "An old man's curse will do you no harm. Henry, this is Mr. Weatherby."

"How do you do?" said Mr. Finch. "Excuse me for being in this filthy state. I had to put out a fire extinguisher."

"Oh, have you actually found it?" Mrs. Finch said. "Where was it, Henry? I hope the poor thing's all right."

"I should say it was in the pink of condition, my dear," Mr. Finch replied. "Some obliging house mover had put it in my briefcase. The briefcase was on the top shelf of the hall closet. I began to pull it down, and as it wasn't properly closed, a great many things began to drop out. The extinguisher just missed my head but fell on its own, and came promptly into action. I think I have killed some of the roses—I had to aim the beastly stuff somewhere—but your extinguisher is none the worse, I believe. I must go and wash. Do sit down, Mr. Weatherby. It's all over now."

"Henry!" Mrs. Finch called after him as he left the room. "Was the corkscrew—Oh, well, he will tell me later. Now, if I could find my list, I could scratch off the extinguisher and the briefcase in one blow. It's a comfort to find that extinguishers work so efficiently, isn't it? Though for the moment I suppose this one has nothing left to work with. Do you often move from one house to another, Mr. Weatherby? It's a very strange experience, but I think if I fell into the way of it, I should enjoy it. It is so enlarging to the mind."

Having got to his feet, Mr. Weatherby had remained there, and now said he really must be going. Mrs. Finch, preceding him into the fall, uttered a glad cry. "Can that be Mr. Harley's hat? And look at this! Isn't this odd?" She pointed to a framed and illuminated text, propped against the legs of a chair. The words of the text were "It is good for me that I have been in trouble."

"Unless Henry had it in college—he had some very queer things then, but of course he has changed a great deal since—I can't account for it," Mrs. Finch said. "Perhaps it was in the house when we came, like the two rag dolls we found in the wine cellar, looking exactly like Sin and Death in *Paradise Unbound*. Is it *your* hat, Mr. Weatherby? I do hope it's none the worse for being extinguished. Goodbye. I am so sorry Cordelia was out. You must come again."

At a safe interval after the door had closed, Cordelia Finch appeared carrying a teapot. "I thought I'd make some fresh tea," she said to her mother, "and I've got some more sandwiches. I thought you might need reviving. My gratitude no words can express, but perhaps a few deeds—What *has* Father been doing?"

The new tea was just being poured out when Mr. Finch came in, smelling of soap, and asked, "Is that freshly made tea or that fellow's leavings?" Cordelia explained that the tea was freshly made. "Thank God!" Mr. Finch said, and then, turning to his wife, he said, "Well, Elinor, what have you been doing all the afternoon?"

"First, I rearranged the poetry shelves," Mrs. Finch said, "and then I had Cordelia's Mr. Weatherby. Cordelia, darling, when you met him, could he talk of anything but his aunt?"

"I don't think he mentioned his aunt."

"Oh, well, no doubt she's died since. That would account for his depression," Mrs. Finch said. "She must have meant a great deal to him. It was impossible to get him to talk about anything else."

An Aging Head

"Goodbye, Aunt Georgie. Ring me up if you feel the slightest need for me. And anyhow, promise to ring me up this evening, to say how you are."

"I promise."

"Or earlier, if you feel inclined to go to bed after tea. Really, it would be wiser to go to bed after tea. In fact, I'm sure you should. So ring me up at Mary's—Barham 257—if it's between three and five. Barham 257. I'd better write it down."

"No, don't bother. She's in the book. And anyhow, I shan't want to go to bed. I'm up now for good and all. Thanks to your nursing, my child." How many more times must I thank you? thought Georgina. And will you never be gone? But the Devil tweaked her tongue and she said, "What will you be doing at Mary's?"

"It's their Friends of the Cathedral evening, you know. So I go in the afternoon to help cut sandwiches."

"I hope you eat some. The laborer is worthy of his hire. Well, I mustn't keep you. Have you got everything?"

"Suitcase, burberry, bronchitis kettle . . . yes, everything. Goodbye, and take care of yourself. Stay indoors."

"I'm coming to wave you goodbye."

"Oh no, you shouldn't. There was such a heavy dew last night, you'll get your feet wet. You are so reckless, I really don't like leaving you alone. Sometimes I wish you'd give up Box Cottage and move to Barham, where I could keep an eye on you. I heard of such a delightful flat in Nelson Place, only a stone's throw from the Close. I suppose you wouldn't—"

Georgina shook her head.

"Well, please take care of yourself. Don't go and have a relapse." Antonia got into her car, started it. Leaning from the window she cried, "Remember hot milk!"

The car vanished round the bend of the lane. With a luxuriating sigh of relief Georgina turned back to her solitude. A breeze shook down a fan of chestnut leaves. The air was full of morning mist and autumnal sun. An unsupervised day extended before her, full of unsupervised activities. There was the kitchen, to be released from Antonia's rearrangements. There was the extra milk to be counter-ordered. There was the lawnmower to be oiled. There was—but she would begin by throwing away that soup.

She began instead by walking round the garden. Though she had only been in bed for a week, at least a month's work seemed to have gathered in the time. Antonia, filling every hour with trays, with improvements, with stratagems for prolonging the lives of pillow-cases and using up stale bread, hadn't done a hand's turn in the garden—and nature, in a last fling of fertility, had been doing a great deal. Now it seemed twice its real size and in process of becoming someone else's garden. Here, however, tilted against the wall to catch the maximum of sun, was the tortoise. She picked him up and delicately scratched his neck. He began to swim dreamily. "I ought to weigh you. If I were Gilbert White, I would certainly weigh you," she said, and put him down again. Her legs felt weak, her remark to the tortoise rang in her head with the unreal loudness of a voice raised in an empty room; but like the tortoise she swam dreamily in satisfaction. She was well again, and alone again, and the sun warmed her skin and presently would warm her vitals.

Something fell with a plop. An apple, of course. She had forgotten the apples. They, too, would have to be dealt with—picked, sorted, stored; even if she only gave them away to the village children, they would have to be picked. Why had she not drawn Antonia's attention to the apples? Apples would have appealed to her; she could have made apple jelly and sold it for much to the poor. Withdrawing her attention from the apples, Georgina fetched her hand fork and settled down to a happy delirium of weeding. Weeding in September is probably a great waste of time, but it stimulates projects for another year. These blocks of snowdrop bulbs she unearthed, for instance, all needing to be broken up and replanted—why not move them to among the hellebores, where they would fill the interval of time between *niger* and *corsicus*? The double lavender primroses, now summering near the water butt, could replace them, unless...But one always lays one's plans for spring and early summer, and leaves the months after July to be sprawled over by annuals already past their best; really, what was needed here was a complete reformation, bold strokes with hollyhocks...Or what about some very dark dahlias and that swarthy, smoky fennel?

When she got up, the weight of the basket with the snowdrop bulbs in it made her stagger. The warmth of the sun had no strength left; she was cold with fatigue as though she had been sluiced with icy water. Somehow she dragged herself as far as the hellebores; somehow she bundled the snowdrops into the ground. The soil was in perfect condition, warmed with summer, moist with those dews Antonia had talked about. Perhaps this was the last perfect gardening day of the year—and here she was, so weakened with Antonia's invalid cookery that she had not the strength to use it. Cursing and defeated, she went indoors. There in the kitchen was Antonia's soup, left ready in a saucepan—ready to be thrown away. She poured it into a bowl and drank it off cold, too tired to get a spoon, too tired even to sit down. Languishing and famishing, she roamed into the larder to see if she could find any more of Antonia's leavings. A card propped against a tray of covered dishes said, "For Your Lunch." Steamed fish, cold in death, watercress, stewed plums, junket...She ate even the junket. There was also coffee in a thermos. Georgina was now sufficiently restored to pour this down the sink and make a new brew. Carrying it into the sitting room, she found another card, saying, "Do Lie Down After Lunch." If it had not been for this, she might have done so.

And it was still only one-fifteen.

Three hours later, Georgina's desolate rambles in search of some congenial occupation that didn't make her back ache brought her face to face with her image in a looking glass. Staring at it, she presently saw that the object confronting her was on the brink of tears. She turned away with a toss of her head. Tea, forsooth! What she needed was red meat and male society; and as a visit to the butcher would not be enough, she would try Eustace Leigh. She had lifted the telephone receiver before she realized that Eustace wouldn't be enough, either. He would twitter about Greece and tell amusing stories of people he knew, and she knew only by name. No, she would try old George, dear old familiar, solid, manly, chop-house

George. He had no gallantry, and his car was a whirlwind of drafts. But he was faithful and admiring and in the past had often asked her to marry him. She would ring him up at his office and tell him how ill she had been, how depleted she felt, how badly she needed a little fun and kindness. Her hand was on the receiver when she paused, and thought again. No, that approach wouldn't do. The days were gone when she could hurl herself on George's faithful heart and be sure of its selfless attention. Rearranging her tactics, rearranging her face—since that is the surest way of rearranging one's voice—she dialed his number and was put through by his clerk.

"George, this is Georgina."

"Hullo, Georgina."

"George, I apologize for ringing you up when you're certain to be busy adding on codicils—but I suddenly felt I must. I've been so worried about you. Are you all right?"

"All right? As far as I know, I'm perfectly all right. Why shouldn't I be, my dear?"

"It's so long since I've seen you. I began to think you might be ill. Are you sure you're all right?"

"Never better in my life. I had a bit of a cold last week, but—"

"Exactly! I knew in my bones there was something wrong. What are you doing about it? Are you taking proper care of yourself? Have you seen a doctor?"

"Good God, no! It was just an ordinary cold. It came, and it went."

"A cold in autumn is never just an ordinary cold. Are you sure it wasn't influenza?"

"Oh, no, I don't for a moment think it was influenza. I only had a temperature for a day—and under a hundred."

"You had a temperature? What else did you have? Did you have a cough?"

"Oh, a bit of a cough." She heard him cough.

"Then I know exactly what you've had. You've had this influenza. Because I've had it myself."

"I say, I'm so sorry. My poor Georgina! As a matter of fact, I thought you sounded rather husky. Did it go to your chest? And did you have that very odd feeling, rather as if you'd swallowed a large piece of cooking apple and it had stuck halfway down?"

Identity of symptoms pointed to the conclusion that what they both needed was rational conversation and underdone steak.

"But, I say, Georgina! Are you sure that you're up to coming out?"

"Oh, yes! Fresh air will do me good."

Whistling "Dalla sua pace," Georgina went to turn on a bath. By the time George arrived she was a renovated Georgina, gay as a kitten with its first mouse.

"Georgina, darling!"

"George, my sweet!"

They embraced with the ease of long habit. When she remembered to hold herself erect, she was the taller of the two. She was now.

"Georgina, I must say, you're marvelous. No one would think you'd had influenza. By the way, did anyone look after you?"

She laughed. "Antonia arrived with the family bronchitis kettle."

During the drive to Barham she told him of Antonia's meatless ministrations and how the very starlings, after their first swoop, had turned away from the grated carrot she had thrown out of the window.

"So what did you do with the next lot?"

"I was brought so low—I ate it."

"My poor carnivore! Never mind, it's all over now. I told Dino we'd begin with oysters."

It occurred to her that she had omitted to ask who had looked after George. However, it was now too late for this; it wouldn't sound spontaneous. They would talk of other things than influenza.

George, in fact, seemed a trifle obsessed with his, referred to it several times, and remarked that when one isn't as young as one was these affairs were a bit of a jolt. But the dinner was admirable, and with the second glass of burgundy he settled down to his responsibilities as a host and began to reinforce the provision of red meat with that other thing she had known she needed—male society. They were both committed gossips, and as most of the people they gossiped about had been known to them for years, it called for a high standard of technique to find more to say and to say it more entertainingly. Exercising the give-and-take of practiced duet players, they knew when to let the other shine forth, when to follow a lead, when to take it. Georgina had more wit, more ingenuity, and a wider range; there was no one she couldn't be amusing about. George's professional honor impeded his universality, but when a death unlocked his silent throat the absurdities and atrocities he could relate and the bland cantabile of his relating was so far beyond anything she could do that she felt all the pleasures of modesty, as well as the pleasures of vanity, when after one of her bravura passages George, in a voice between a choke and a squeal, exclaimed, "My dear Georgina! My dear Georgina! I don't believe a word of it." But this was not the only nourishment, nor the most invigorating, that George's male society afforded; the thing she essentially craved for and fed upon was the contrast between George's mind and her own. Where she was brilliant and malicious, he was placidly savage. Where she went to work with a dancing, prancing stiletto, George would aim one accurate condemnation and chop a head off. Several heads fell that evening, some of them heads she esteemed or had a weakness for or would have saved up for a finer examination of the evidence; but seeing them roll, she thrilled with the realization that George, in his stupid infallible way, was right. She was enjoying herself so much, and doing so well with her womanly stiletto, that it was a shock to be told that she was looking tired and should be taken home. "You mustn't go and have a relapse." The injunction had a familiar ring. Who else had...Of course, Antonia.

"George, do you like hot milk?"

"It's one of my passions. Didn't you know? Especially with skin on it."

"So do Tartars. I expect you're a Tartar at heart. Well, when we're back I'll make you a brimming blue-and-white mug of hot milk—with a skin as tough as Pamela Hathaway's."

There was not much conversation during the drive back. George was not a conversing driver. As they rounded the bend of the lane, they saw a car drawn up at Georgina's gate. It was empty. As they walked up the path, they saw someone come from the porch and run toward them.

"Aunt Georgie! Oh, thank God! What happened? Are you all right?"

"George has been giving me dinner at Nicolino's, and now he's brought me back. George, you know Antonia, don't you?"

"I was so worried when you didn't ring me up—because you'd promised you would, you know—"

"It went clean out of my head. I must be growing quite senile."

"—and when there was no answer when I tried to ring you, I decided the only thing to do was to come. And then I found I couldn't get in. And I had just decided I must break a window when

I saw a car stop and heard you coming up the path. Oh, Aunt Georgie, I'm so thankful, so thankful!"

"Well, now we'll go in by the door. George has a horrible cough, he oughtn't to be standing about."

"It's Antonia who has been standing about," remarked George. "She's shivering. I'm going to light your fire."

The fire had been laid several days before. It was slow to kindle, appearing to partake in the general feeling of constraint.

"One's glad of a fire in the evening now," said Antonia.

"Yes, isn't one?" replied George.

They knelt before it side by side, Antonia tempting its appetite with twigs, George puffing with the bellows.

"I think perhaps if we made a hole here with the poker..."

"Good idea!"

A Boy Scout, a Girl Guide—it was not the end to her evening that Georgina had intended. She went out to get glasses and bottles. Where on earth had Antonia put the vodka?—for on inspection the bottle she picked up proved to be rennet. From the sitting room came sounds of encouragement, of growing confidence, of disillusionment. Then silence. Then a roar. They were doing the newspaper trick, and would set fire to the chimney. "Remember my thatch," she said, glancing in.

George looked round. "It's perfectly all right, Georgina. I know how to manage it." At the same moment the newspaper burst into flame. George leaped up and trampled on it. Then came a smell of singeing; Antonia began to pat the top of her head. "Good Lord, have I set fire to your hair?" he exclaimed.

"Oh, it's nothing," Antonia said. "Frizzy hair like mine catches fire so easily."

"I suppose it does." George himself was bald, so there was even less reason why he should speak in the tone of one pondering a new light on the universe.

Georgina retired. When she came back with the tray, they were reclining from their labors on the hearthrug. The Girl Guide had ash on her nose, the Boy Scout was wheezing.

"What will you drink, children? Whiskey, vodka? Some orange juice for you, Antonia?"

"But where is my hot milk? You promised me hot milk, Georgina."

Affronted by this unchivalrous reminder, Georgina contented herself by suavely supposing Antonia would like hot milk, too.

"I'd love some. Let me make it!" She half rose, thought better of it, sank down again; as Georgina left the room, she heard Antonia say, "But why don't you try iodine? Sailors never catch cold."

The kitchen was warm and exclusive. With leisurely movements, Georgina took a bottle of milk from the refrigerator, selected two suitable mugs, opened the lid of the Aga stove, and took down a heavy saucepan. For one does not spend a lifetime enjoying English literature without being made aware of the nature and capabilities of milk. Milk, proverbially mild, is a devil when roused by boiling, and in a moment will writhe out of the pan and spread itself all over the place—waiting with fiendish malice till your back is turned before doing so. Profiting by the strenuously acquired wisdom of novelists and essayists, Georgina did not intend to be caught like this. She put the saucepan on the hot plate and emptied the bottle of milk into it. Half the amount would have been quite enough, but she had enjoyed the gesture of emptying, a gesture at once lavish and contemptuous. They would just have to wait rather longer— what of that? Besides, presumably the skin would be all that much thicker. Words rose in her mind: "If you want to have proper skin on your boiled milk, it's hopeless to use less than a pint." Other words floated in from the sitting room—soothing, diagnosing words from Antonia to George, who liberally as to a midwife was declaring the state of his bronchial tubes. George would be all right if he didn't eat so much—but Antonia didn't raise this issue. Meanwhile, the milk lay quietly in its saucepan.

An hour ago, heads had been rolling, and Canon Toller, pierced in a dozen places, had been tossed aside, the sawdust trickling from his reputation as an apostle to youth. Now George was maundering on the hearthrug and she was in the kitchen—alone, aging, disregarded, haggard with fatigue, still not over her influenza but expected to be as strong as a horse, with the garden full of apples and the sink full of dirty plates and dishes—waiting for milk to come to the boil. The voices had become lower, more confidential—bunions, probably; the milk was unchanged except that from time to time a vague, sneering frown seemed to cross its smooth brow. Antonia said something not perfectly audible about it perhaps getting worse if you lived alone. George, perfectly audible, replied, "The truth is, Georgina's totally selfish." And at the same moment the milk exploded and spread itself all over the top of the Aga.

Georgina filled the two mugs and carried them into the sitting room and set them down without a word, sincerely hoping her guests would scald themselves. They did not. Antonia sipped, and said how delicious. George sipped, and asked if he could have some sugar in his.

"Oh, do you take sugar in yours?" Antonia said, plainly making a note of it.

"And with porridge. But there I like it brown," said George, as plainly expecting a note to be made.

And when they had emptied their mugs they thanked her and went away—musingly, and slightly flushed.

She heard their diminishing voices, and their lingering farewells. She heard George cough, and Antonia deplore. She heard them start their cars and drive away. Presently they would set out on an entirely novel way of life, hyphenated into George-and-Antonia—one of those late marriages that at first seem so surprising and soon after seem so natural that one can't imagine why they did not happen earlier. And she would go on pretty much as usual—an aunt to Antonia, to George an old acquaintance, a headless phantom. They would always treat her with kindness, and Antonia would unfailingly remember her birthday and ask her to lunch.

Love

"No. There's no telephone," said the long-legged young woman. "It seemed more important to have drains, so we chose drains. We couldn't afford both at once."

"Far better to have drains," said Dinnie.

"Yes, that was what we felt. You see, it needed so much doing to it. It was a farm cottage once, but no one had lived in it for years. But we fell in love with it, we felt we must rescue it. We did think of calling it Cinderella Cottage, but Jim said it would be whimsical."

"I like Meadow Cottage much better." Dinnie looked out of the window at the calm Cambridgeshire landscape, cows under elm trees, shorn midsummer fields dotted with trusses of hay. It wasn't in the least what they were looking for, this rather self-conscious Meadow Cottage—but perhaps as a pro tem? It smelled of wood smoke . . . Wood smoke always makes one sentimental.

"It will be sad for you to leave it, when you've made it so charming—even if it's only for a couple of years."

"Nothing would make us, if it weren't for Jim having to go to Rhode Island to print *The Anatomy of Melancholy*."

A queer reversal, thought Avery. Twenty years ago, young couples were writing arresting new books. Now they were all typographers, doing limited editions of classics. Twenty years ago, too, young couples used to be approximately the same height.

"What rent—" began Dinnie. Avery broke in; he could see she was dangerously drawn toward Meadow Cottage. "Which press?" he asked.

At the same moment a door opened, a coffee tray was put down with a clatter, and the short stout young man said, "I hope you'll excuse me, but the house is on fire."

He darted away, leaving the door open behind him. The young woman hurried after him. A waft of flame came down the wide chimney like a goblin, flared, vanished. Avery shut the door and the window opening on the calm landscape.

Dinnie was on her feet. She had emptied a log basket and was filling it with their Staffordshire chimney ornaments.

"You get down the pictures, Avery. We can't just sit here fiddling. We'll take everything we can outside, the poor creatures!"

He unhooked the pictures and stacked them. Dinnie had opened a bureau drawer. It was full to overflowing. So was the next drawer, and the next.

"There never is anything to put anything in in an emergency," she said in the fractious voice of one hardened to insult.

"And all these books," said Avery. "Folios and the Lord knows what." He had a pile of them in his arms as he spoke, his chin resting on the topmost. As he spoke the midmost books escaped and cascaded onto the floor.

"Use the curtains."

The curtains were on a rustic string. He wrenched them down and the books were bundled up in them.

"Now for it! Let's hope the passage isn't blazing."

As they opened the door, another goblin of flame darted down the chimney. The passage was filled with smoke. The young man peered over the stair rail.

"We're taking some of your belongings into the garden," said Avery.

"To be on the safe side," added Dinnie.

The young man said, "Thanks a lot," choked, and disappeared.

"Have a wet blanket," Dinnie shouted after him.

Thick smoke drifted over the garden. Tufts of burning straw floated down. Overhead was a noise like the swarming of innumerable hornets, and looking up they saw flames cringing among the thatch.

"Her linen! The linen cupboard is sure to be upstairs." Dinnie ran back to the house. The young man came running downstairs, holding a picture. They collided, and went on their ways.

"We can get out that bureau between us," said Avery to the young man. "This is bloody for you. I suppose it's a fuse. It's usually a fuse." The bureau was massy. They paused in the passage to set it down.

"Where's your wife?" asked Avery.

The young man replied that she was putting things into cartons and that he didn't know where they would be if it hadn't been for Mrs.— "But I don't know your name."

"Kelso."

A pile of sheets fell on them. "I believe all women feel like that about bed linen," said Avery, the first to recover.

"Not in Switzerland," said the young man. "In Switzerland, people use paper sheets."

"Good God!"

They picked up the bureau and when out with it, returned for more furniture. As they carried out a settee, a hail of shoes descended. Dinnie was at an upper window, encircled with roses below, flames above.

"Dinnie! Come down."

"Mrs. Kelso, you oughtn't to stay up there."

"I'm putting Sheila's clothes in pillowcases," she said. There was a smudge on her cheek. The smudge and her wide-brimmed hat made her look absurdly girlish—childish, rather. For the thousandth time in his life Avery reflected that he was the hearthrug of a fireside sphinx. How did she know the young woman was called Sheila? How had the hat stayed on?

"Dinnie! *Come down!*"

Sheila came out, carrying a glass rolling pin, a miscellany of kitchen equipment, and an umbrella. She stood silent as a dumbwaiter while Jim unloaded her. "We've got each other," she said despairingly when he removed the umbrella. Another pillowcase thumped down, and another. It struck Avery that Jim and Sheila had got considerably more than each other—and that so far Dinnie had done nothing to insure Jim more than the clothes he stood up in.

"Sheila, where do you keep—" Her voice leaped an octave. "Look! It's coming!" Avery started back; he had been severely bruised by a flying alarm clock. "It's coming! It's seen us. We're saved!"

A lorry reeled across the meadow, shedding baled hay with every lurch. Two men jumped off.

"Got a ladder, Mister? No? Well, if you'll clear this stuff out of the way and not mind what happens to your hedge, we'll drive right in and do it from there. Do it in no time."

A space was cleared, the lorry was backed in and maneuvered into position. Standing on it, the two men clawed away the burning thatch with their long-handled forks. The beams, the blackened rooftree appeared. Vast quantities of thatch smoldered on the ground, and the men went to and fro kicking the sparks out of it.

"There," said the older man. "You'll be all right now. This cottage has been needing a red jacket for the last fifty years, but it won't have one this time." He laughed kindheartedly and contemptuously. The younger man said he'd see what he could do about putting his hand on some hayrick tarpaulins. They drove off. As the noise of the lorry died away, there was an extraordinary silence; the hornets swarmed no longer. Dinnie walked out of the house as though she were going to a royal garden party, glanced at Sheila, and put her arms round her. By the time Jim and Avery had carried everything back, she had collected the remains of the picnic lunch from the car and was feeding Sheila on cucumber sandwiches.

"What a strange day," she mused as Avery drove westward. "One never knows what one's setting out for. That's why I had my smelling salts. Poor girl! Not that I liked either of them very much. Those nice men would have gone away without a grateful sixpence if it hadn't been for you. But they'll soon forget it when they're in Oregon."

"Rhode Island."

"Rhode Island? Well, somewhere, anyhow. Her comb hadn't been cleaned for days, but her shoes were handmade, so they can't be penniless. I wonder what the rent would have been. Not that we would have taken the place—I could see you didn't like it."

"I believe you did."

"Only to think about. As a stopgap, you know, till we find something permanent we both like—with a moat, perhaps. I've always liked the idea of a moat."

What a strange wife, mused Avery after she had fallen asleep beside him in the hotel bedroom; which was no longer alien since it had her smell. Next year would be their silver wedding; the two sons she had borne him were out in the world; within three years, he would retire and live on beside her in that unknown house which they were already prospecting for. It would not long remain unknown: he would know without thinking where its electric-light switches were, the progress of the shadows across its walls, the trees —beech or conifer or palisade of aspens—he would see from its windows, the noise of the wind in its chimneys, the names of the local tradesmen. And Dinnie would be as unknown as ever—as kind, as heartless, as capable, as fallible, as mysterious. And he would be taking her for granted, since there was nothing else for it, it is what one settles to. But as for knowing her—he might as well hope to know her dreams. She stirred, moved closer, fitted herself into the curve of his buttocks.

"Dinnie."

No answer.

"Stay, Corydon, Thou Swain"

THE MOON was at her full, and the Choral Society of Wells in Somerset was holding a practice. Moonshine had to be consulted, for many of the singers lived outside the town and would not venture from their homes by night unless they could see the ruts and puddles. Mr. Mulready, however, was independent of the moon; he lived in the market place, and a gas lamp shown in at his bedroom window until 10:30 P.M., when all the street lamps gave a little jump and died.

Mr. Mulready was a draper. He lived above his shop, though he was sufficiently well-to-do to live, had he wished to do so, in a villa near the station; and this evidence of proper feeling made him much esteemed by the local gentry. He was a small, bald-headed, puggy man, and could sing both bass and alto. What was more, he could read music at sight. These good gifts he employed weekly at the Bethel Chapel, and it was said that Mr. Bulmer, a vicar-choral, had fervently attempted Mr. Mulready's conversion, in order that he might sing in the Cathedral, especially that alto solo in an anthem by Samuel Sebastian Wesley which declares that, "as for the gods of the heathen, they are, are, are but IDOLS"—a sneering chromatic phrase which would ring finely under the stone arches if delivered by the rescued Dissenter, but which that bleating old Philpot could never sing in tune.

But Mr. Mulready was faithful to Bethel, as much from social as from religious convictions; for, as he said, he was a Baptist born and dipped, and it never did for people to pretend to be what their neighbors knew full well they were not. The Choral Society was another matter: he had been a member of it for nearly twenty years, and he knew most of its repertory by heart.

The piece they practiced this evening was a madrigal by John Wilbye: "Stay, Corydon, Thou Swain." He had sung in it many times before; he knew every note of it; but this did not lessen his pleasure—indeed, it increased it; for he was able to enjoy its beauty undistracted by the sheet of music that Mr. Fair, his neighbor bass, jerked up and down before him in time to the music.

Yet tonight he was destined to hear the old favorite with new ears.

"Thy nymph is light and shadowlike," sang the first sopranos, coming in on high G, and the second sopranos took up the phrase a fifth lower. All of a sudden Mr. Mulready found himself wondering about nymphs, and wondering, too, in a very serious and pertinacious way. He had never to his knowledge given a thought to these strange beings before, and yet it now seemed to him that he had an idea of them both clear and pleasant—as though perhaps in childhood he had been taken to see one as a treat.

He wished to see a nymph again: not from motives of curiosity, not because he thought a nymph would be a pretty sight to gaze at, not for any reasonable, pleasure-seeking reason—for how could anyone entertain a rational wish about a mythological fancy? What he felt was more than a whim; it was an earnest desire, a mental craving somehow to re-create a bright image that Time had once timelessly given, and then by course of time effaced.

Even as he sang he looked round on the lady members of the Choral Society to see if they could afford him any clue as to the looks of a nymph. One by one he rejected them. Miss Fair was as pretty a girl as you could wish to see, young Mrs. Buckley had a complexion as red and white as the rosebud chintz in his shop, little Jenny Davy was as light as a feather and as ruthless as a kitten—yet none of these answered to his idea of a nymph. She would be quieter, somehow—more ladylike.

So next he studied the ladies, the real ladies who came from the Cathedral Close or from the country houses round about. They were no more helpful. The Reverend Miss Perceval (so he thought of her) had something rather promising about her small pale ears; but, poor young lady, how she did stoop! And as for Mrs. Hamlyn, whom there had been all that talk about, she was a highflyer, sure enough, but nothing like a nymph. Her nose was too large.

Not like any member of the Choral Society, not like his dead wife, not like his two daughters, not like any woman he had ever seen—how did it happen, then, that in his mind's eye there should be this image of a nymph which he was now trying to confirm by looks of flesh and blood? A picture? On an almanac, perhaps; some of the wholesale firms sent out very handsome ones to the trade. But a picture was flat, a picture was dead: no picture could have become so living to him as this projection of a nymph which he couldn't quite see, but which was none the less present in his thought; for otherwise how could he reject so certainly all these unnymphlike ladies?

"Thy nymph is light and shadowlike."

The words haunted him as he walked home, and he hummed the phrase over and over as he sat at supper, with a kind daughter on either hand. As he kissed Sophy goodnight, he thought how cool a nymph's forehead would be. "Light." Light-footed, that must mean, not light-complexioned; for his nymph was dark—at any rate, she had dark hair. The words ran into a new order: "Light-and-shadow-like"—wavering, rippling, as the light bubbles through the shadow of a bough that sways in a spring breeze. As one has a word on the tip of one's tongue, so Mr. Mulready had a nymph on the tip of his imagination. And for one moment, just as he blew out the candle and resigned his senses to the bed, he thought he had caught her. Alas, she was gone again in a flash, and he was left with a new perplexity; for now it seemed to him that instead of having seen her long ago he had seen her quite recently, so that her image was indistinct and elusive not because Time had effaced it, but because Time had not yet enforced it, leaving it still a faint penciling, a sketch.

In the morning he had forgotten these thoughts; but he was soon to remember them again, for when he walked into the shop, there, behind the polished counter and laying out rolls of flannel and sarcenet, was his nymph. He recognized her as one recognizes a melody; her looks, her gestures, fulfilled everything he had sought for overnight, as though a tune that he had tried unavailingly to recall had come back into his head complete. With the recognition came the identification; his mind's nymph was Miss Edna Cave, the young lady who sold staylaces and suchlike female oddments in a dark secluded corner of his shop that in high-flown moments he referred to as the "haberdashery department." There she was, and, what was even stranger to him, there she had been for a couple of months. She was a very respectable, quiet-spoken girl, and a good worker, though she had somehow a rather languid air. He remembered wondering when he engaged her if she were anemic, and if she would be strong enough to lift down the heavy boxes from the shelves. And from then till this moment he had scarcely given her a thought, perhaps because of her very merits as a satisfactory worker and respectable young person.

He wanted to think of her now, to examine her in this new and exciting aspect of a discovery. But it was market day, and the shop soon filled with customers. He was kept busy and could scarcely steal a glance at his nymph until the moment came for him to put up the shutters and for her to put on her hat and gloves.

"You look a little tired, Miss Cave. It's been a busy day, I'm sure. There's more than twenty pounds in the till."

"I'm not tired, really," replied the nymph. "Only a little sleepy. It's the spring, I expect. These first warm days often make me feel a little queer."

"You should go out more," said Mr. Mulready. "Have you a bicycle?"

"Yes, I've got a bicycle."

"I'll tell you what you should do. Tomorrow is early closing. Now, will you come out for a ride?"

"I must say that Annie will come too," he thought; but before he could utter the words the nymph had answered, "Thank you, Mr. Mulready. I should like to very much."

Even so, he fully intended to ask Annie, or, if not Annie, then Sophy. It would be nice for her to have the company of girls her own age—bright, friendly girls like his two. But on the morrow he learned from their talk at breakfast that they proposed to go off early in the forenoon to shop in Bath, and would not be back till late. Apparently it had all been settled long ago, even to the hats they were going to buy: a pink chip for Annie, and for Sophy a leghorn with a wreath of white roses.

"You won't mind, will you, Pa? Mrs. Creak will see to your tea."

"I don't know whether I shall want tea, my dear. I was thinking of going out for a ride with—"

The shop bell rang. A little boy had been sent in a great hurry for some narrow black elastic, and Mr. Mulready did not have another chance of a word with his daughters. It seemed as though Fate had taken the affair in hand. It would be a pity to disappoint the poor thing, and on such a lovely day, too. But would it be right to ride with her alone? He tried to quiet his scruples by remembering the innocence of his intentions and the number of years that he had been a respectable widower. Yet in a small town one cannot be too careful; and he would be sorry to compromise a nymph. Besides, it would be dull work for her, riding through the spring lanes with such an old fogy as he; she would enjoy herself more when the girls could come too.

Just before closing time Miss Cave approached him.

"Would it be as convenient, Mr. Mulready, if we don't start till about five? Mother wants me to help with the ironing."

He would have spoken then, but suddenly she raised her eyes and said, "I am looking forward to it so much."

No, he could not make difficulties now. After that stint of ironing, the hot room, the heavy sheets to handle and fold, a bicycle ride would be just what she needed.

It was after five when they set out.

"Where shall we go, Miss Cave? Is there anywhere you specially fancy?"

"I should like to go—" she had a low voice and spoke with a curious slight lisp, her speech seeming as it were to rustle—"I should like to go by Glastonbury to that wood called Merley Wood."

"It's rather a rough road, you know. Have you been there before?"

"No. But I've heard of it; and I have often wanted to go there."

He knew the wood she spoke of; that is, he had often passed below it, had heard it murmuring aloofly to itself, had seen the long shadow it stretched down to the road. He was not a fearful man; yet for some reason he did not much care to pass Merley Wood toward dusk. It gave him an uneasy feeling in his back, and he had once declared in the safety of jest that he wouldn't walk through it—no, not for a five-pound note. But if Miss Cave wanted to go there, that was another matter. When one has a nymph vouchsafed one for a whole evening one does not boggle over details. He was extremely happy and excited at the thought of such a shy and rare being becoming his companion. Now he would really be able to watch, to discover, to make sure of her—or, rather, of the nymph-idea she represented for him. Whatever she did or said would be, he felt sure, the right, the revealing thing. He had already a general idea how a nymph would behave: she would be rather quiet, and take a great interest in flowers.

Yet when Miss Cave, riding ahead of him, suddenly jumped off her bicycle, he cried out, "Is it a puncture?"

She did not answer. It seemed that she had not heard him. She stood looking into the hedge and smiling at whatever it was she saw there.

"White violets," she said softly. And then she smiled again, and gently nodded her head, as though between them and her there were some especial understanding. Mr. Mulready also nodded—nodded in approval. Yes, it was just as it should be; a nymph would certainly behave thus. It was a pretty sight, and he hoped she would do it again.

She did, jumping off her bicycle, as other people jump off when they see a friend, to greet a flicker of windflowers in an ash coppice, a new growth of Queen Anne's lace—very light and feathery, yet eminently vigorous with the thrusting strength of its sappy green stems—a handful of wild white hyacinths that some child must have gathered and then thrown down in the road to die. But these she took up without any word at all, and for a moment she looked almost severe as she considered them, drooping limply and exhaling their heavy smell of sweetness and untimely death, before she laid them among the grasses at the side of the road.

"It's a thing I don't like at all," said Mr. Mulready, "picking flowers just to throw down."

"No more don't I!"

He was surprised at the passion in her voice. He had never heard her speak so vehemently—nor, it occurred to him, in such a rustic way. But in a moment she was her ordinary self again, had mounted her bicycle and was pedaling on before him with her white thread gloves on the handlebars. She rode very fast for a girl of her build. He had quite an ado to keep up with her, and by the time they reached Merley Wood he was hot, and glad of a respite.

They ran their machines into the field below the wood and laid them down under a group of blossoming thorns. A blackthorn hedge straggled up the slope toward the wood; the blossom was beginning to go over, and drifts of tarnished snow lay under the bushes. But in the shadow of the wood, where the sun had not penetrated, the thorn trees were at the perfection of their bloom. They were very old trees, gnarled, and tufted with greenish-gray moss, dry and dead-colored. It did not seem possible that those angular boughs should have put out the lacework of milky blossoms, each a blunt star, each with its little pointed pink star within it. It seemed rather as though light had rested upon the dead boughs and turned into blossom.

Behind this flowery rampart the wood rose up—sycamore, and sad spruce, and larches sighing and swaying their young green overhead. It was certainly a mournful wood, but Mr. Mulready could not now imagine why he had thought it to be a frightening one. Now that he was within it, walking about with Miss Cave, he thought of it as a gentle place. Presently they sat down side by side, and, having sat a little while, lay back, as everyone does, sooner or later, in a wood, to stare up at the tree tops waving so high above them.

Mr. Mulready watched till he began to feel a trifle sick. He sat up again, and as he did so it occurred to him that he had come out this evening to watch, not larches, but a nymph. And this was a good moment to begin; for she lay staring upward as though she had forgotten his presence—he could look as much as he pleased without being ill-mannered.

First, then, how slender she was, and how supple; for she lay among the wood sorrel as though lying on the ground could never make her stiff, could never give her rheumatism. And next? What struck him next? Her pallor—she was as white as the thorn blossom. But down here at the foot of the trees the light was dim and watery, as if it floated down to them through still, shadowed water. That was why she looked so pale. No real woman had naturally such a moonlight look.

And then? Her hair, which he now saw was not black, as he had believed, but the color of very dark earth? Her eyes, which were a bright, spangled hazel? Her wide, thin mouth; the line of her jaw, traveling from the small chin to an ear that was quite as fine as Miss Perceval's? He noticed all these things, but he knew that there was something else, something more significant than any of these. Of course. Her silence. For, except for that one outburst over the wild hyacinths, she had scarcely put two words together during the whole evening. Yet you wouldn't call her uncompanionable. When he had spoken she had answered him, though not in words, now he came to think of it; but assenting with sighs of contentment, and acquiescent murmurs, and even little grunts—matching her speech, as it were, to that of the whispering and faintly creaking trees around them.

How still she lay! He could hear her light breathing among the sounds of the breathing wood. Had it not been for her eyes, still open and fixed upon the treetops, he would have said she slept.

Outside the woods, among the thorns, a blackbird had begun his vespers; and the rays of the sun slanted in and turned the larch stems pink. Time was getting on; they should soon be thinking of the ride home. When she woke, when she came out of her waking dream, he would take out his watch tactfully.

But suddenly she turned to him, saying, "I am so happy here."

One couldn't answer that by taking out one's watch: it wouldn't be manners.

He made a nice reply—hoped they might have another ride soon. A second blackbird was answering the first from the farther side of the wood. Their voices traveled through the solitary still dusk where these two sat, unguessed-at and secluded as though they lay at the bottom of a shadowy pool.

"Listen to those two chaps," said Mr. Mulready. "There's singing for you! Are you fond of music?"

"I'm afraid not. At least, I don't care for the piano."

He wondered if he should tell her how a phrase from a piece of music had brought them here together. But perhaps she wouldn't understand, for he was a poor hand at explanations; and perhaps it might wound her feelings if it came out that he had invited her for such a queer reason.

"Thy nymph is light and shadowlike." He began to hum to himself, softly and strayingly. Music has a different meaning, a different beauty, out of doors.

The sun had faded out of the wood, the stems of the larches were grown silvery, the wood sorrel they lay upon lost all earthly color, became gray, became almost black. The smell of the thorn blossom drifted into the wood. Every moment it became more intense and more searching, as though it were the smell of the moonlight.

The nymph sat up and looked about her. She put her hands to her forehead as though to wipe away a dream. Then, shaking her head, she rose and began to walk out of the wood. Mr. Mulready picked up her hat and gloves and followed her. When he came to the edge of the wood he caught his breath and started. The thorn blossom shone so in the moonlight that it looked unearthly. The landscape lay before him, undulating to the horizon in swaths of gray and silver like the swaths of mown hay. Down in the field he could see the two bicycles. Their spokes glittered in the moonlight. The dew was falling, and they would be rusted.

He began to descend the slope, but stopped again; for the nymph delayed. She had turned back toward the thorn trees at the edge of the wood. She stood beside them, quite still, gazing at them as she had gazed at the white violets, earlier in the day—gazing as though, rather than seeing them, she were listening to them. Now she began to walk toward them, very slowly. She put out her hands. He thought that she was going to break off a spray, and, remembering the country belief that whoever takes home blackthorn blossom carries death into the house, he had a confused idea that he must call to her, warn her, tell her not to. And then in a moment she had disappeared.

He saw it happen, but he could not believe his eyes. He told himself that she must have slipped round to the other side of the brake, and as he ran back across the dewy grass he kept on saying, "Oh no, oh no! It can't be! It can't!"

But though he called, and searched, and fought his way into the strong mass of the thorn thicket, frantically believing that she had got in somehow and fallen there in a faint, there was no sign of her. She was gone. With his own eyes he had seen her vanish.

Breathless, and scratched all over, and trembling, at last he sat down on the grass; and, covering his eyes with his bleeding hands, he began to whimper like a lost child. But it was she—she who was lost! And as he abandoned his mind to an acceptance of what had happened he began to forecast in a confused terror all the things that would happen next: a scandal, nobody believing him; Edna's mother weeping and wailing, and perhaps bringing an action; his customers leaving him; his daughters disgraced and turning from him; misery, shame, ruin! The scent from the thorn trees flowed out over him. He caught hold of a branch and clasped it in his arms, awkwardly, as though he would embrace it. The thorns ran into his flesh and the petals slipped floating down on to the ground. "Oh, come back, come back!" he implored. But there was no answer, no sound, except the nightingales singing in the wood.

Afternoon in Summer

HE BECAME aware that Sally had emerged from her book and was about to say something.

"Murder is an occupational risk for prostitutes."

"Hmmm," said he, clinging to the thread of his calculations. They grew so engrossing that when next she spoke it took him by surprise.

"And for wives, too—though not so much so."

Inwardly assenting, Willie asked, "What on earth are you reading now?"

"A book about all the murders committed in the last thirty years. I got it from the public library."

"Is it interesting?"

"Yes. In rather a stark way. Just facts and sentences."

"Sounds enthralling."

"But murder is not so much of an occupational risk for murderers. I mean, they mostly aren't hanged. Of course, that's a good thing."

He looked at Sally's sleek flaxen head, now bent over her book again. Though he was still young, still a student, he was a year older than she and found her artless sophistications touching. It was as though the mental processes beneath that hood of silken hair were as sleek, as smoothly disposed, as childishly combed and clean.

He worked on. She read. The alarm clock ticked. After an hour had passed he realized that it was two-thirty and that he was unfed.

"Are there any cases in your nice book about husbands who ate their wives? I'd like to know their sentences."

"Oh, Willie, are you hungry?"

Her gaze rested on him, calmly attentive, as if this were another interesting social phenomenon. She put a marker in the book and closed it. He cleared his papers off the table and laid them on the floor. The dwelling they had rented for the summer vacation was advertised as "self-contained." It was so self-contained that the only place for their bicycles was in the bathroom-kitchenette. Skirting the bicycles, Sally now opened a small refrigerator, and considered its contents: a heel of cheese, some rye biscuit, one tomato. She put these on a tray and after further consideration added salt.

The tomato was scrupulously shared between them. It seemed of an Oriental richness and succulence.

"I had a shopping list. But when I was halfway there this morning I remembered the bloody grocer shuts on Thursdays."

"May Hell be hot for him," said Willie, mildly. "Never mind, I'll tell you what we'll do. We'll cycle along the road toward Cowfold, and have an enormous tea at The Goat."

"That inn we passed with the roses?"

"*And* the check curtains."

"*And* the frogs."

"*And* the milking stool."

There was no such adventitious rusticity about the dacha they had rented from Miss Hobson, professor of Lit. Hum. at Willie's red-brick university. Plain as a packing case, with an air of having lost all interest in going further, it stood at the end of a long flinty track across flinty fields of sugar beet. "Wonderful views of the sky," Miss Hobson had remarked.

With only one puncture, they reached the crossroads and turned toward Cowfold. The sun beat on their backs, midges stuck to their faces. Strong Indian tea and strawberries and cream, thought Sally. Strong Indian tea, plum cake, and ham sandwiches, thought Willie. The Goat appeared in the heavens, motionless on its signpost against a glaring blue sky. There were the roses, there was the lily pond, with concrete frogs. They dismounted. Swaying with hunger and heatstroke, they walked up the crazy-paving path. On the doors was a notice: "NO TEAS."

Sally moaned and sank down on the milking stool.

Willie looked at his watch. "Twenty to five," he said. "They're legally bound to open at six. We'll kill time till then. Think of those poor wretches who go to the moon."

"And there'll be a church somewhere. We haven't passed one, so we shall come to one. Churches are cool."

When they had soaked their handkerchiefs in the lily pond and washed off the midges, they rode on, came to the church, went in, sat down. Its proportions were ideal: it was larger than Miss Hobson's packing case, not so large as the face of nature. And somewhere about it a bell was ringing in a calm liturgical way.

"I can't understand why people don't make more use of their churches."

"Sectarianism," said Willie. "I don't suppose anyone will come near this place till Harvest Festival."

"Which is phallic, isn't it?"

At that moment an approaching voice remarked, "We brought

nothing into this world, and it is certain we can carry nothing out. The Lord gave and the Lord hath taken away; blessed be the name of the Lord."

It was also certain that they could not escape; for a surpliced clergyman came in, preceding a coffin borne on the shoulders of six heated men in black cloth suits, and followed by a small group of partially blackened mourners. The coffin was put down on trestles and its wreaths adjusted, the mourners, stumbling over hassocks, filed into the front pews, the clergyman glided into the reading desk and began: "I said, I will take heed to my ways: that I offend not in my tongue," to which the clerk responded hastily, "I will keep my mouth as it were with a bridle, while the ungodly is in my sight."

It seemed to Sally that the clerk's glance aimed these words at her bare head and her blue slacks; in fact, Mr. Hicks was scanning the congregation with a professional eye for mourners whose grief might get out of hand. The corpse had been bad enough. At no time did the Reverend favor long-departed parishioners being brought back to take up room that the churchyard could ill spare, to cause upheavals in family graves that the course of time had flattened into an easy surface for the grass-cutter, to bring nearer the dreaded day of an extension encroaching on the rectory kitchen garden. The least they could do was to be punctual; and Charles Joliffe was almost three hours overdue, the hearse breaking down and none of them rightly knowing the way. *I became dumb and opened not... When thou with rebukes dost chasten...* Me to the life, thought Mr. Hicks—the responses snatched from his lips before he'd half finished them. He would have his work cut out to keep up with Reverend, crackling ahead like a gorse fire. And if Reverend was like this in a verse and verse psalm, what wouldn't he be in the Epistle, with the reins thrown over his neck and the smell of his stable, which in this case was his tea, not to say his dry martini, firing his heels through the Fifteenth Corinthians?

. . . *forasmuch-as-ye-know-that-your-labour-is-not-in-vain-in-the-Lord.*

The coffin was lifted; its direction was reversed in a peculiar dance by the bearers. Preceded by the clergyman, followed by the mourners, it loomed down the aisle, it went past. One of the mourners paused beside Sally and Willie. "Thank you so much for coming," she said. "It was so kind of you." She hurried after the rest.

"That was a near thing," said Willie. Sally nodded. He got up and began to read the pamphlets displayed on a table near the entrance. Presently he went to the door and peered out. "Still at it," he mouthed; and wandered off to read mural tablets in the chancel. There was the sound of cars being started up. Running down the aisle where the coffin had gone so cumbrously, he whisked her into the porch just as the clergyman came in by a side door, pulling off his surplice.

"Do you think he's a vicar or a rector?" said Sally, averting her eyes from the raw earth, the tumbled wreaths. "They ought to wear some distinguishing badge, like pips in the Army. And, of course, there are curates." Her brave conversational voice snapped like a fiddle string. "Oh Willie, Willie! It's so awful." She burst into tears and clung to him. He patted her shoulder, smoothed her burrowing head, and started at a smart new headstone. *Helena, Beloved Wife of Hubert Wilkins. Aged 71. At Rest.*

It only left Sally fifty more.

"So awful. Why can't one just be cremated without having to die?"

It seemed a quite rational aspiration.

"The chances of a sudden death must be going up by leaps and bounds," he said. "Come, my darling, let's get out of this blackmailing churchyard."

They found a lane and wandered along it till they came to a gate into a meadow. In the meadow was a large sycamore. They lay down in its shade. Forgetting that they were mortal, forgetting that they were hungry, not noticing that they were lying above an ants' nest, they began to make love. He licked the delicious salt off her cheeks, she nibbled his nose. They fell asleep, and woke, vaguely wondering why they were there, and made love again. He cut an "S" and a "W" on the bole of the tree and framed them in a heart and finished off the heart with an arrow; and when they had vowed to come back every year on the seventeenth of July, they bicycled to The Goat and drank dog's-nose and ate small porkpies of the meanest possible description with such abstracted greed that, as the barman said later to the waitress, it was plain to see what those two had been up to.

A Scent of Roses

In 1917 Howard Wilkinson, at the age of ten, became his mother's only comfort. At first, he rather liked it: he wore a black armband and slept in her bed.

Before the third anniversary of his father's soldierly death, the moderate liking had waned to a dulled acceptance of being an adjunct to her daily life. Her life was extremely daily; she was as repetitive as the calendar. Waking on a Monday, as surely as he foresaw that Sunday's joint would be served cold with a salad, on Tuesday be a hash or a Lancashire hotpot, he knew that on May 12th, his Aunt Maud's birthday, he would hear how shockingly Maud's hair kept falling out; on July 19th, Reggie's wedding day, that Mrs. Reggie had a touch of the tarbrush. Quarter days, bringing a statement from the bank, were accompanied by having every reason to be suspicious of the bank manager; the narrative of the final exposure of Basil's machinations with old Fladgate was told at Halloween. The year was embossed with regular surprises, at which he had to be surprised, and regular excursions: Lake Ullswater (honeymoon), Isle of Man (bluebells), Morecambe Bay (shrimps), and Bishops Totterby, where

Mrs. Wilkinson spent her happy, simple girlhood. For these, and for all other mercies, he had to be duly thankful.

Mrs. Wilkinson was also thankful—thankful for her Howard's devotion, steadiness, pleasure in the simple things of life, sunny disposition, clean mind, and the entire confidence between them. These were public thanksgivings—at home she was captious and demanding. They made him a laughingstock among his schoolfellows, who addressed him as Bed Socks and asked if his bowels had worked yet; for the public thanksgivings were qualified by regrets that Howard had inherited his father's cold feet and sluggish liver.

Shakespeareanly speaking, Howard's liver was cold, too. He took his education in sexuality, theoretical and applied, as listlessly as though it were in English history. Mrs. Wilkinson, doing her part later, was rather more successful. She chose an excursion to Lake Ullswater (honeymoon) to explain how simply and beautifully he was begun there, stressing that he must always respect women, because, though marriage is a beautiful relationship, the woman's part in it is painful and uncongenial, and only put up with for the sake of the little life to come. This quite new idea animated Howard. One day, he would assert himself, and get a bit of his own back.

On second thoughts, he returned to his intention of being a monk. As a monk, he would be quit of responsibility, there would be no women to please or pain, no little lives to worry him, he would call his cell his own, pray and eat at regular hours, fast in Lent, wear sandals, and be respected by everyone. When the moment was ripe, he would break it to his mother. But not till he was twenty-one. Meanwhile, he took a course in metallurgy, and got a post with Joskins, a local firm.

At twenty-four, he was still living at home, where Mrs. Wilkinson, who was beginning to feel her age, spent many interesting hours wondering whom she would leave him to. Hearing that on the whole he would be happiest with Myra Leadbetter, Howard felt he must take a hand in his own disposal, and selected a clerk in the accountancy department. She had no immediate relations, parted her hair in the middle, and was old enough not to be in any romantic hurry. On a wet Sunday, she jilted him. To regain his self-esteem he visited a brothel, where he got on better than he expected. On a later visit he overstayed any credibility of his pretext of working overtime. His mother switched her gaze from the clock-face. "Howard!" (When angry, she pronounced it "How-word," like clods falling on a coffin.) "You smell of cheap scent." They glared at each other like two confronting animals. No more was said. From that justifying moment he began to feel faintly affectionate toward her, took her to the cinema from time to time, tolerated her fuss, her praises, her fits of ill temper and her hats, and by dint of feeling superior to her came to think of her as a credit to him. She died, leaving him considerably more than he expected. She also left him an interest in life—his grandfather's stamp collection. It had been totally forgotten, and was rather a good one.

Joskins was now part of a combine. In 1938 he got himself transferred to headquarters and moved to London.

Two years later, he wished he had not done so. The Blitz was not his mother; he could not outglare it. He was continually afraid. But as he was totally lacking in adrenaline, he acquired the reputation of being imperturbable. As he had flat feet and was shortsighted, he was able to go on being indispensable. He was twice evicted from his lodgings by blast from a nearby hit, and resorted miserably to the cellerage beneath his place of work. Rats resorted there, too. When there was a lull, he came back to the surface and found a bed-sitting room in Pimlico. After the lull came the flying bombs.

There was no knowing where they would drop, and conversation at the eating house where he had his supper that evening in August was dominated by two statisticians, one arguing that this diminished the risk of being killed, the other that it increased it. He was walking back through the natural dark of blacked-out London when he heard the noise, the summer-cockchafer approach of a V-1, persisting above the clatter of people running to get into the street shelter. It dropped on the public house at the corner. The air was full of dust, bricks, earth, splintered wood, broken glass; he was thumped and jostled; a woman clung to him and screamed in his face. Her open, screaming mouth was bare as a baby's. Slates, chimney pots, bits of masonry dislodged by the blast were falling all round. A swaying housefront suddenly fell out, like a toy. There was a strong smell of gas. Wardens and police made their way through the crowd, saying, "Move away, please. Room for the ambulance."

He wandered back to his lodging house. The door had been blown in; a bath blocked the hallway. A faint light powdered down from a gash in the roof. Enough of the bottom flight of stairs remained for him to mount partway up it. From there he got a sight of his room. It was recognizably his, and the legs of a piano—the second-floor piano he had execrated—projected into it. Somewhere there was a slow dripping of water. He went back and sat down on the doorstep. The dark throng of people that had seemed part of the explosion thinned away. "It *would* go and drop on a public," said a voice. Another voice replied that there had been a delivery that same morning. By this date, loss of liquor was more significant than loss of life. Other voices complained of the way wardens bossed you into rest centers as if they were sweeping you under the mat. The water dripped on. An ambulance clanged its way out of hearing. He fell into a miserable drowse. His head dropped forward, and as it did so he became aware of a pain in his cheek. He put his hand to the place; his fingers stumbled on a splinter of glass. He pulled it out and was holding his handkerchief to the gush of blood that followed it when a small beam of light wandered over him.

"You're bleeding."

A helmet, the bulk of a trousered uniform, a woman's voice... one of those air-raid wardens who would sweep him into a rest center.

"It's nothing. A bit of glass, and I've pulled it out."

"Lucky it didn't get your eye."

"Many killed?"

"Five for certain. There may be more underneath."

Talking made the blood flow faster. He mopped. The saturated handkerchief was stiffening.

"You must get stitched at the First Aid Post—second turning on the right. That handkerchief's no good now. Take this." She opened her coat, dived into her bosom. It was as if she had opened the coat on a different world, a world of warmth and sleep and riches. The handkerchief was soft as a rose petal and smelled of roses.

"I can't bleed on this; it's too expensive."

"Nonsense."

He went on expostulating. His mother, who liked things dainty, had made him aware of best handkerchiefs sprinkled with lavender water, and this was far beyond her finest.

"Very well," the woman said. Her voice was tolerant and fatigued, as if she had been humoring fractious children all day. "If you feel like that, you can return it. This is my address. Now go off and get seen to."

The First Aid Post smelled of blood and disinfectant. But when he got away, the handkerchief still retained its smell of another world. He scarcely connected it with the woman. When it came back from the cleaners smelling of the cleaners, he retrieved the card from his pocket. Miss Millie Roberts, and an address off the Fulham Road. As he passed the Cancer Hospital he noticed the flower seller and bought six carnations.

She came to the door of her flat wearing a dressing gown. If it had not been for the smell of roses, he would not have known it was she.

"How kind of you—and carnations, too." She pressed her nose into the jaded flowers. There was the noise of a man's shoes being kicked off.

"I'm sorry I'm engaged just now. Perhaps you'll look in tomorrow. No, not tomorrow; the evening after. Tomorrow I'm on duty." Catch me, he thought, going away indignantly. It was easy to see what she was.

But on the evening of the aftermorrow he went again. The woman in the helmet who had preceded the woman in a dressing gown stood in the way of his intention. The helmet hung just inside the door, and she was wearing a black dress and a cardigan; and though she was evidently expecting him, it was rather as though she were expecting him to have come about the gas. For a moment, he wished he had and could escape on it. But already she had got him to her sitting room, had offered him a cigarette, was talking about the weather and the war. Her glance rested on his cheek. He wished he had taken off the strip of pink plaster. A black patch would have looked less unheroic. She asked how the cut was getting on, and he replied, thankful to have a subject for conversation, that it was mending and no longer festered—adding that he was always a bad healer.

"This should help," she said; and while he was expecting her to produce a tube of ointment she leaned forward and kissed his cheek.

. . .

During the next ten years he loved her with all his cold heart. She never changed her scent, so it seemed to him she grew no older. She aroused no jealousy in him, and no particular desire. She contented him. He was one of her Regulars—she concentrated on Regulars. He visited her once a fortnight, which was just right. He kept a pair of slippers there, and when he arrived they had been put out for him. He brought an evening paper.

No doubt there were other pairs of slippers; he vaguely pictured a sort of filing cabinet. At times he vaguely speculated about the other Regulars, not all of whom might be so peaceably satisfied as he. As well as the filing cabinet, was there a cupboard where she kept whips, chains, outsize women's underclothes? He inquired a little, but did not press his inquiries: "Some people have the funniest notions what it's all about," she said. "You can have no idea." Her eyes under the unchanging symmetry of their plucked brows were candid as a cat's, and he remained with no heightened ideas. Her plump white skin bruised easily. He averted his recognition from the bruises; they were professional, even honorable, scars, fleeting medals acquired in the course of duty. His real curiosity directed itself as his mother's would have done: who was she, where did she come from, how much money had she got, did she pay her bills weekly or let them run on? The answers to his mother's more imperious questions he knew already. She was not respectable, her teeth were her own, she was irreproachably clean.

For some time he took it that she was socially a cut above him: her manner, her clothes, her appurtenances implied an accustomed superiority; there was nothing flashy or artistic. It was partly a relief, partly a disappointment to learn that her father had been a postman. Like Howard, she was born and bred in the provinces, though on the opposite side of England—Lincolnshire against his Staffordshire.

Like him, she was early fatherless; but she was one of five sisters, and their mother had been high-spirited and indulgent: "larky" was the word she used. The house was noisy with girls and canaries— gifts from Uncle Bartle in Norfolk, who bred them as a hobby. His nieces went to him for their yearly holiday, boating and sailing on the Broads, where he kept a boatyard for summer visitors. A happiness such as he had never felt was reflected on him as she talked of the boatyard and the pocket money the five girls made, scampering barefoot on errands for the houseboat people, swabbing decks, selling early-morning mushrooms. Two of them had gone the same way as herself—Ivy, who was the beauty and died after an abortion, and Cindy, the runt, now married to a rich man in Canada and opening church fêtes.

It was so real to her, this incompatible past, that she spoke of it as though the rough pleasures, the exploits, the eight half-crowns tossed into her dinghy from the deck of the towering black-sailed wherry were still at her command. She told stories of local hauntings—the mourning coach with a headless driver, the hanged Abbot of St. Benet's, Old Shuck the enormous goblin dog—as though she believed them. She turned to the rasping singsong of the dialect as easily as turning over in bed, used local idioms, said "Bless your flesh," called him "Bor." Bore he might be; but it had shocked him that she should choose a moment of endearment to tell him so.

For the rest, she told him nothing, and he hadn't much to tell about himself. Lovemaking over, he read his evening paper and she went on with her petit point. Occasionally he read her bits from the Stock Exchange column about the rise or fall of her investments— she was shrewd and prudent in placing her money—or racing tips, for she liked a gamble. Time went on, methodical as the petit point.

84

She contented him. It was what he wanted; it was all he asked for; above all, he was sure of it.

The thought of giving her pleasure never occurred to him. He gave her chocolates at Christmas, flowers at intervals (but she was always well supplied with flowers), his clothing coupons—she had asked for them. Once, a sudden ambition entered him. She lived on a plateau of middle age, always using the same scent and never seeming to grow older; but she must have a birthday somewhere about in the year. Birthdays are to be celebrated, presents must be a surprise. Allowing an artful interval, he asked the date of her birthday, the name of her scent. It was a French name, and she wrote it down for him. The date lay conveniently near the day of his next visit. His chemist sold perfumes, some with French names, but none with this name. He went to another, and another. It gave him a quickened sense of manly pride to be taking so much trouble to please Millie. He went to perfumery departments in stores; he went to small crystalline shops in the West End. Some had never heard of it, others did not stock it. Only on the eve of his visit did a gray-haired shopwoman with silver fingernails read the name as though it were a commonplace to her, unlock a glass cupboard, and from the top shelf reach down an oblong navy-blue package—one of several, all of the same size and looking as unvoluptuous as wardresses. But the name on the label was right. "How much?" he asked, thinking he might ask her to wrap it ornamentally, with bows. "Seven guineas," she said, as though he were uneducated not to know it.

Trembling at this step into the world Millie's bosom had opened to him when he sat bleeding on the doorstep, he blinked and paid. Afterward, he reflected that he knew more about scent than his mother did, and had got a bit of his own back.

For he still bore his mother a grudge, and for anything that went wrong with him still blamed her: shrimps made him sick; hand-knitted socks gave him nettle rash. The passage of time merely enforced her, for he was impaled on her anniversaries. On the twelfth of May his Aunt Maud shed her hair, the last Sunday in August haled him to Bishops Totterby; on March 15th poor old Pickwick, the faithful terrier, died in agonies. As he had inherited her retentive mind, he went on accumulating anniversaries of his own. He knew the length of service of everybody in the firm; he remembered wedding days whether or no he was invited to them; deaths were engraved on him as though on marble. He was a ledger of anniversaries. He asserted himself by not observing them. The bottle of scent for Millie was different. He was positively glad she had been born on April 17th and that on August 28th her little beam of light had caught him as he sat bleeding on the doorstep of No. 47.

The tenth anniversary was past. He had been aware of it because it was an anniversary, but not till later did he realize that a tenth anniversary, an anniversary in double figures, calls for a special acknowledgment: that he ought to give Millie a present; that he would like to do so. He was standing outside a jeweler's window, looking at an assortment of brooches on a black velvet pad (he had decided that a brooch would be best, though his first impulse had been a ring), when a girl tweaked his sleeve. "Thinking of giving me a present, Romeo?" He walked away. She followed him. To escape her importunities, he signaled a passing taxi. It slowed, he hurried toward it, slipped off the pavement's edge, lost his balance . . . There was a clamor of screaming brakes, bellowing horns, voices. He tried to get up, and a lacerating pain felled him.

He was still hopping on one leg when five days later he crutched himself to her door.

"Why, what's been happening to you? And didn't you get my telephone message? Sit down and tell me all about it... Wait a minute, I'll just fetch your slippers."

As he had not brought a present, he did not go into the whole story. He told how the taxi-driver had insisted on driving him to the hospital, how long he had waited before anyone came to attend to him, how he had been wheeled to the X-ray department and again kept waiting there, how easily it could have been a Pott's compound fracture.

She listened, questioned, sympathized, put the slipper on his uninjured foot as solicitously as though it had been the injured one.

"About all I can do for you today, I suppose," she said.

In fact, it was all he wanted: her warmth, her composure, her painless familiarity, her scent. He leaned back and sighed with pleasure. "I'm glad I came. Do you know, I nearly didn't come. It's the first time I've been out."

"So that's why you didn't get my message. The girl at your office said you hadn't come in yet but she'd give it to you when you did. She might have had the sense to post it on. But she didn't."

There had been a telephone message. His slippers had not been put out. He began to think.

"What was the message? Are you expecting someone else?"

"No, no, Bor! All that's over and done with. I'm retiring."

But why was she retiring? She was as good as ever.

"That's why I telephoned. To ask you to dine with me instead. I thought we'd have a little farewell celebration."

Had she come into a fortune?

"Is this a new idea, this retiring?"

87

"New idea? We've been saving up for it for years, Fred and me."

"Fred?"

"Fred Larter. He's the wine waiter at the East Anglia Hotel. He was odd-job boy at the boatyard, twiddled outboard engines, patched sails. He could put his hand to anything. Uncle Bartle paid him five bob a week, and always said he'd go far—be it London, be it the devil. He was the first one who ever kissed me proper, was Boy Fred. Chased me into the water and kissed me among the swans. You'd never think it to see him now, so responsible and stately. Nor me, neither."

It was as though the hoyden virgin stood there, drenched with joy and defiant. Her professional competence was gone. She suddenly looked much older and unrecognizably young.

"I'm sure I hope you'll be happy," he said at last.

"We'll be happy, all right! We're going to live in France, in the brandy country. Fred's bought the house. He got it through a friend in the trade. It's nightingales everywhere, he says. And roses."

She appeared to catch sight of him from a distance. "If you should happen to want an introduction, there's a friend of mine who'd be just what—"

"No!"

It terrified him to hear the fury in his voice.

Tebic

When the airliner detached itself from English soil, and Rosalind, the Warburtons' only child, was off with a husband and a trousseau to settle in Australia, Humphrey Warburton was aware of a profound and yet quite trifling sense of relief, which he could not account for until Lydia, coming out of a muse, remarked that it would seem very odd to have grandchildren who as a matter of course ate plum pudding in the dog days—and did he suppose they set fire to it?

"Set fire to what, my dear?"

"Christmas plum pudding—in Australia."

Christmas. That was it. That was why he was feeling relieved. It was annulled—his ignominious bondage to a recollection of how, one Christmas when a miniature tallboy, perfect in every detail, one of his best finds, had proved half an inch too tall to fit into Rosalind's dolls' house, Rosalind had referred to "that silly old Santa Claus." One may laugh off such things, but if one is a man like Humphrey Warburton one continues to brood over them, and all subsequent presents to Rosalind were, as far as he was concerned, poisoned at the source. But henceforward Rosalind would receive his presents in another hemisphere, and he would be able to give his whole mind to filling the Christmas stocking for Lydia—Lydia, whom he had so discerningly chosen when to people of less connoisseurship she was still just one of Archdeacon Barnard's pigtailed daughters, and whom he had never ceased to love, and whose tastes he could be sure of, and who was so easy to compliment at any season.

One reason he could be sure of Lydia's tastes was that they were so engagingly eclectic—as if some part of her were still feasting on lemon drops in the rectory schoolroom. It was also very engaging that Lydia should be so honorable that for some weeks before Christmas she always entered the room humming with artificial spontaneity and keeping her gaze directed on the ceiling, in case she should surprise Humphrey wrapping something up. In point of fact, Humphrey began amassing things for Lydia's stocking so far in advance that he was exposed to surprise from January onwards, and by the time they were given, all wrapped up with such artifice that not a revealing contour protruded, he was often as much astonished as she. In the stocking of Christmas 1957, for instance, the glass top hat, the Portuguese reliquary with its half-dozen minute splinters of bone in cut-paper ruffs reposing on crumples of blue velvet under a crystal dome, and the new patent kind of clothesbrush warranted to take up cats' hairs, all came as novelties to him. So did a small round sky-blue plastic container.

"How I love and adore little round boxes," said Lydia, smoothing out the silver paper it had been swathed in. "How does it open? What's inside?" She turned it over. "Look, here's the head of Athene embossed on its back. It's not a tape measure, for there's nothing to pull out. Oh, it's got its name on it! Tebic.... Humphrey, what is Tebic? What does it do?"

"Its duty—as Woolworth expects of it. Now go on to something else; you're still only halfway down."

He could not be more explicit because for the life of him he could not recollect where he had bought Tebic, or when, or what it was for. Ashamed to disclose this, he waited until Lydia had got to a vanilla bean, and then began the unobtrusive tidying in the course of which he proposed to smuggle Tebic out of sight and into the wastepaper basket.

"I've always thought it so unenterprising of people with hot-houses not to grow their own vanilla," she was saying. "Do you suppose it climbs, or is it more like a horned poppy? No, Humphrey, *not* that sprigged paper! It's just what I need for lining the satinwood desk. Goodness! Do you know what you nearly did? Rolled up Tebic and threw it away. Why should it be scorned because it came from Woolworth?"

Lydia's chivalry had been aroused, and all was lost. When the stocking presents were laid out for review, Tebic was in the front row, between the reliquary and an Indian miniature of a lasciviously squinting rajah. All being lost, he had to make a clean breast of it.

"I have no idea what it's for, and I don't even remember where I got it. All I know is that I have been concealing it from you for months."

"I'd love it for that alone. And I'm sure that when we've found out what it's meant to do, it will be an answer to prayer. Perhaps it's for withering away that immovable tape people *will* do up parcels with—in which case, what a godsend! Or for putting in damp cupboards, or mending china, or adding vitamins to soups."

"I am positive it is nothing to do with food," said Humphrey.

"Well, that's a step towards the truth. Perhaps— Humphrey!

where are my glasses? It says something in very small letters round the rim. 'Do not open till required for use.' Oh!"

She replaced it with deference between the rajah and the reliquary. "Perhaps it's something immensely powerful for putting out fires with. Anyhow, we won't open it."

Humphrey wished to hear no more of Tebic. Tebic threatened to prey on his mind, a trumpery variant of the miniature tallboy. But perhaps it would only prey passingly; for during the first weeks of new years Lydia was accustomed to discard with great tact and disingenuity (the children of the late Archdeacon Barnard had been schooled never to tamper with the truth, but had been permitted, in cases of extremity, to draw a veil) any stocking presents she had not really liked.

Thus, the reliquary was sent to Rosalind, on the ground that one of the worst things about life in the colonies must be that one so seldom saw anything with associations; Humphrey hoped that, in a like spirit, Tebic might be bestowed on old Mr. Tovey, who complained that there was no mystery left in modern life, or on one of those recurrent jumble sales held for the upkeep of the Village Hall, a fabric that Humphrey, who was an architect, would gladly have assisted to destroy. But on the first of February Tebic again met his eye, looking even more ostentatiously blue now that the sun had returned from fetching new lust from Capricorn. It was on the upstairs windowsill where Lydia kept her special geraniums. Could it be that she had run its purpose to earth, and that it was one of those concentrated tonics that indoor gardeners poke into flowerpots?

He looked at it more closely and saw that the lid had not been removed. And suddenly Tebic no longer arraigned him for an inadequacy, a lapse, a horrid little piece of ill manners he had hoped to forget about. Quite the contrary. The boot was plainly on the other leg. For here was Lydia, who had been so quick to get rid of that really charming reliquary just because she could not adjust herself to a few fragments of unpedigreed bone, cherishing with an equal degree of superstition a ghastly little box of sky-blue plastic, while at the same time—so indifferent was she to his gifts, or by now probably bored to death by them—making no attempt to discover the use of what it contained. He was still looking out of the window and trying to master a sense of injury when Lydia came along the passage carrying Bianca to her kittens.

"That cat of yours has no maternal feeling," he said.

Lydia looked momentarily startled, but retorted, "Neither would you have if they were getting their teeth."

Bianca, under the usual female misapprehension that men are susceptible to flattery, scrambled onto his shoulder and purred in his ear. Disregarding her, he continued, "This object, Lydia—this object which has just caught my eye—how long has it been here?"

"Oh, for some time. I put it there to remind me to send back the library books."

"And did it?"

"Ten days ago," she said virtuously. "But that's not all. Now it's there to remind me to tell you a rather unpleasant piece of news. Perhaps I'll do it now. I've had a letter from Mary Fitzgerald, and she wants to come to lunch. Look us up, she said, but it means lunch. And lunch will have to mean tea. I know it ought to mean asking her to stay the night, but I cannot, cannot endure being told the latest way to suck eggs and how to remove bloodstains from old baths for longer than four hours at a stretch. So I said Thursday week."

"Thursday week. I shall be out all day. Lydia, if you must keep a *memento mori* on this window sill, why can't you find something that isn't an eyesore?"

"Why are you so set against poor Tebic? I admit it's rather flaunting, but you did buy it for me and keep it all those months. Even if we don't know what to use it for, it would be a pity not to use it. Besides, I like wondering what's inside."

"Have you taken any steps to find out what's inside, Lydia? Have you asked anyone?"

She shook her head.

"Well, you'd better ask Mary Fitzgerald."

"Heaven forbid! I'd sooner perish."

"But haven't you even any theories about it? It's not like you to be so totally without speculation, my love."

To call her his love reminded him, even at a moment when he might more properly have addressed her as his hate, how entirely his happiness depended on loving her. So he handed her Bianca, since just then he had nothing else to give, and said encouragingly, "That head of Athene on the back, for instance—that ought to be a clue. What do you associate with Athene?"

"Owls."

He laughed, and felt safe. Tebic's brief power to sow discord between them was at an end.

But snakes that have missed their strike renew the poison under their fangs, and when an object has shown itself potentially malign, it is best to be on the safe side and not leave it lying about to ripen a second assault. Humphrey decided to find some other remembrancer to sit on the windowsill; he would find it between now and Valentine's Day, so that it could accompany the ritual gloves.

Unfortunately, just then an extinct cesspit at Coldkettle manifested itself under the half-built Gothic-style summerhouse that was to be the main feature of a garden layout Humphrey had designed for a Mr. Clark, who had handsomely stepped in to save Coldkettle—that splendid example of secular Pugin—from demolition and was doing it thoroughly. So Humphrey had to travel into Northumberland to deal with the problems arising from the pit, and he stayed on in order to oversee the rather ticklish restoration of a gatehouse that the War Office in 1940 had converted into a machine-gun post; and, as Coldkettle had been commissioned by one of the Victorian eccentrics as a sort of personal La Trappe, and stood on the moors miles from anywhere, which was no doubt the reason why the War Office thought that crucial engagements would take place around it, Humphrey was unable to do any shopping, and had to come home without a substitute for Tebic. He came home on a Wednesday, and in his satisfaction at being home he conceived an entirely new system on which to arrange his books; and by midday on Thursday all the books were on the study floor, and everything was in a state of creative chaos, at which point Lydia looked in and said, "You remember, don't you, that you are going to be out all day? Because Mary Fitzgerald will be here at any moment."

"Good God! Well, in that case there's no time to change my plans. I shall lurk here, and later on you can creep in with something on a tray."

"But then I shan't be able to explain that you were obliged to go out."

"Tell the truth and shame the Devil, then. Say I am arranging my books."

"I'm sorry, Humphrey, but that won't do. For one thing, it might hurt her feelings. For another, she'd come in and help you."

"Tell her I'm ill—something infectious but not prostrating. Tell her I've got pinkeye... Very well, then, tell her I *think* I've got pinkeye. Surely your conscience could go so far as that. It's got an enormous balance in hand; it would never feel the difference."

He was still trying to outmaneuver Archdeacon Barnard's sturdy shade when Mary Fitzgerald proclaimed her presence in the house. "Lydia! Lydia! Here I am. I let myself in, to save trouble."

"These labor-saving devices!" Lydia exclaimed. She set her teeth, arranged a smile over them, and left the room.

Lydia was right, and lunch would mean tea; for Mary announced that she would take off her hat and just run a comb through her hair. As they went upstairs, he opened the study door a chink and listened, since at least he ought to know if he was developing pinkeye. Gabble-gabble, gabble-gabble. Then came a loud, glad shriek.

"Tebic! So you are a Tebic addict, too."

Nothing is created without purpose, said Humphrey to himself. Mary Fitzgerald knew about Tebic, and presently he would partake in that knowledge. For Lydia, reared in strict regard for truth, could scarcely pretend to be an addict to something she knew nothing about. Besides, why shouldn't she ask? There is nothing humiliating in an honest admission of ignorance.

The ensuing silence was fractional, though to his impatience it seemed endless. Then he heard Lydia say—and her voice was round and warm and glowing as a pigeon's breast—"I can't imagine myself without it."

He gave a shout of laughter.

Having thus discovered himself, there was nothing for it; he had to go in to lunch. And between lunch and tea Mary Fitzgerald insisted on arranging his books for him, grouping them by height, which would make it much easier to dust them.

A Flying Start

YOUNG Mr. Harington was paying one of his usual studious visits to the Abbey Antique Galleries and had as usual brought Mrs. Harington with him. Seeing them come in, the assistant, mindful of a previous recommendation, unobtrusively withdrew; the gentleman was one of those customers, like the pot in the proverb, who won't come to the boil if they are watched. Mr. Harington had settled to his studies, and Mrs. Harington, who couldn't positively withdraw, was giving an appearance of having done so, gracefully killing time with the patch boxes and vinaigrettes displayed on the rosewood sofa table, and eventually rewarded by finding something she could study, too. She stood patiently, cradling it in her hand. Once or twice, she held it out, saying, "Look, Richard. Isn't this rather..." But Richard was absorbed in the decision whether or not to buy the *églomisé* mirror, and did not turn his head.

If a poet or artist had happened to be walking down Abbey Street and had glanced in at the window that framed Richard and Lizzie Harington amid the dusk and glitter of the showroom like two elegant fish poised tail downward in a rather overfurnished aquarium, he might have wondered why anybody should be interested in antiques when the Abbey Galleries contained two such strikingly handsome specimens of the contemporary. The third denizen of the aquarium (a crab, not a fish, and therefore stationed, not poised), Mr. Edom, the gallery owner, was lurking behind an Empire harp, waiting for Mr. Harington to make up his mind. The young gentleman was a distinguished customer, one who paid on the nail and scorned to bargain; but it did not do to hurry him.

There was a sudden stir in the aquarium. Richard had taken the wallet out of his pocket. But a moment later he put it back again, and with the coquettish flick of a fish moved away to examine a George II coffeepot. His examination was appreciative but did not go deep. Noticing this, Mrs. Harington came forward, holding out her hand. "Look, Richard. Isn't this rather charming?"

On her palm lay a very small enameled locket, shaped like a heart; against a scarlet background and framed by a band of seed pearls was the head, in full face, of a gray cat with a pretty expression. "I suppose it's Victorian," she said.

Mr. Edom, coming forward in his turn, said, "Second Empire."

Richard Harington gave the locket a brief but careful scrutiny. "I don't like it."

Her lovely, tranquil countenance registered no shade of disappointment, of protest, of private disagreement. Without a word, she replaced the locket on the velvet-lined show tray whence she had taken it, and began to turn over a portfolio of prints.

She's not out of quite the same drawer as he, thought Mr. Edom —a fact that he had for some time suspected. Too tactful. Poor young lady, she wouldn't get her locket! A shame, really, since she had been so taken with it. But, of course, young Mr. Harington was absolutely right; the locket would have looked quite unsuitable—

trivial, and even slightly disgraceful—attached to that classically long, full, white neck. It wasn't that Mr. Harington grudged his lovely Lizzie a pleasure, didn't love to decorate her: the necklace of white jade, the set of French paste, the Nattier fan—no end to the things he had bought her; though lately the ardor of his choosings had turned more strongly to the furnishings of his son and heir. But if you possess both flawless taste and a flawlessly lovely young wife, you are bound to feel as a connoisseur as well as a husband. A matter of what you might call sacred and profane love, thought Mr. Edom; they can't be expected to curl up under the same blanket. That is what flawless taste brings you to, rendering you unable to enjoy both the draped beauty and the plump dreamy charmer who leans over the wellhead as though she were smiling at the reflection of her breasts. Flawless taste—an excellent thing in a customer but outright ruin to any art dealer if he once allows it to dictate to him.

Meanwhile Mr. Harington had left the coffeepot, paused awhile for another survey of the Waterford comports he had looked at last time and wouldn't get this time, either; and returned to the *églomisé* mirror. There he stood, gazing at it with the whole power of his sight—and not even noticing the reflection of himself that it gave back. I hope he gets it, thought the dealer. He deserves it.

And at that moment the door opened and a lady came in. Could anything be more unfortunate? Wringing his hands behind his back, Mr. Edom approached her in silence.

"Have you got a pair of Staffordshire prophets?"

"No, Madam. I have no Staffordshire of any description."

Short of spitting in her face, he could scarcely have made himself more repelling. Trembling with thankfulness, he saw her go away.

Mrs. Harington had strayed her way into the more miscellaneous assortment at the back of the gallery. Mr. Harington was still fixed before the *églomisé* mirror. Time went on.

"I'll have it." Raising his voice, he called, "Lizzie! Come and look at this. Shall we have it?"

"Oh yes! It's an enchantment. I've been longing for you to get it."

It reflected her as though she were standing in the doorway of a trellised arbor. Mr. Edom came sidling into the background of the picture. "So have I, Mrs. Harington. I knew it was Mr. Harington's piece. So much so that whenever a London dealer has come in I've stepped it up by another fifty guineas. Defended it with my life, you might say."

Out came the wallet again, and a neatly folded check was drawn from it and filled in with young Mr. Harington's usual care. Whether he made out his checks for a sum of one figure or, as in this case, three, he wrote them with the same deliberation, read them over with the same care, and checked them against the receipt. Meanwhile, Mrs. Harington had gone in search of her gloves, which she had put down, she said, somewhere or other.

"I think you left them on the sofa table, Mrs. Harington."

"So I did! Mr. Edom, you're wonderful. You're a falcon. You notice everything."

Together they left the gallery, he with his receipt, she with the heart-shaped locket. Mr. Edom had noticed this, too.

Having summoned back the assistant, he got out his ledger and wrote against the *églomisé* mirror, "R. Harington Esq. 4 V 62," and against the locket the word "Lost," with no date. He felt no animus; indeed, he felt a kind of admiration, and even a degree of tenderness. She had known what she wanted; she had secured it. She might become a collector yet. What would she go in for? Cats, or heart-shaped objects? Both are much collected, so in either event she had made a flying start. Heart-shaped objects, cats . . . Since she was not invigilated by flawless taste, her collection might end by being more illustrious, and certainly more interesting, than her husband's accumulation of virtuoso pieces. But the little locket would not appear in it; she would keep that strictly to herself. *Deep in my soul the something secret dwells*—a poem by Byron that he could not altogether remember. *Lonely and lost to light for evermore.* Then something about a sepulchral lamp. He reflected with pleasure that he had undertaken to supervise the delivery of the mirror that same evening. He wanted to see her again, to view her in this new and interesting light of larceny.

But he was disappointed; she was, he learned, upstairs, putting her little boy to bed.

It was several weeks before he saw her again, on another of young Mr. Harington's studious visits to the gallery. It was during a spell of very hot weather, and she carried the Nattier fan. But even before he recognized the fan he saw that a change had taken place; for now her lovely, tranquil countenance had acquired a pretty expression.

English Mosaic

WHEN a stranger walks into an antique shop, an experienced dealer doesn't need to ask himself whether the entrant has come to buy or hopes to sell. Mr. Edom, who kept the Abbey Antique Galleries, in St. John Street, could tell at a glance, or even without glancing—by a footfall, by the timbre of a cough—what was in the air. In the case of those who came to buy, he could usually make a good guess as to what they were after; apart from dealers and runners, who stick out, as he was wont to remark, like good deeds in a naughty world, there is the clockwork type, the satinwood type, the like-it-quaints. But who might bring in what to sell remained a mystery, and always would. Buyers express their own preferences, sellers the preferences of others—of those they have inherited from, or accidentally acquired from (you wouldn't believe what treasures can be left behind in a lodging house)—or perhaps the preferences of those whom they have obliged by taking a settlement in kind. Even in the case of things that have been stolen, the prior preference echoes on, like the cry of jarred crystal, through the automatic vulgarity of the thief's notion of what may be worth stealing; and as such preferences are sometimes quite exquisite, checking one's purchases against the lists of stolen valuables that the police issue to the trade can be extremely painful. A dealer, however chastened by professionalism, remains human and has preferences, too. Something he really fancies comes along. He buys, only to find he must notify the authorities and see it pass from his hands. Altogether, as Mr. Edom often confided to his assistant, trading with unprofessional venders, never knowing what they won't bring in, and having to judge from what they've brought what else they might have up their sleeve, is a tricky business, not to say incalculable.

To the young lady who came as a replacement when the assistant was swept off to the hospital for a month's treatment, Mr. Edom had nothing whatsoever to confide. Her qualifications and references were all anyone could ask, and the London agency that produced her assured him he was lucky to get such a nonpareil at such short notice. But after a couple of days, he knew he couldn't stomach her. She was a Miss Know-All.

So, the first time he had to leave her alone in the Galleries, it gave him considerable pleasure to say that if a seller came in and wouldn't wait for his return, she was to make out a receipt of deposit, take the seller's name and address, and bid him call later for Mr. Edom's decision. "No comments, please, Miss Hartley. Just the routine acceptance pending a possible offer."

"But if it's something obviously impossible?"

"Even so, if you don't mind."

That she had minded with fury was plain when he came back and found her blandly gloating over two rock-garden rabbits, a grouse claw mounted as a brooch, and a large framed photogravure of Wedded Love. Being master in his own establishment, he took her down by remarking with suavity that the time wasn't yet ripe for these. This went home nicely. For the next half hour there wasn't a whisper of omniscience out of her, so absorbed was she in brooding on her wrongs and thinking of all the retorts she might have made if she had thought of them in time. When another absence and another visitor with something to sell gave her a fresh opportunity to express her resentment by displaying with the utmost prominence on a show table a proffered Staffordshire Duke of Wellington hot from Czechoslovakia whose steed trampled on a *bocage* of soap-bubble iridescence, he used a variant of the same technique, dwelling with tutorial tact on all the reasons that would have justified her in viewing the ornament with mistrust. "As I don't for a moment doubt you must have done, Miss Hartley."

"Well, I should hope so!"

"Exactly, exactly! With all your knowledge, I was sure you would."

She could be stifled, but not for long. Only by wringing her plump young neck could he have silenced her affability, her fellow-expert airs, her sprightly comments on his customers, her mosquito persistence in teaching him his own business. It was torment to be under the same ceiling with her. However, trade was slack, and though it was a choice of evils—for Miss Hartley was visibly pleased to be left in charge, and pleasing Miss Hartley was no pleasure to him—he contrived to be out pretty often, sweetening his returns by airy visions of finding she had done something he could be disagreeable about. She never had. After reporting on her blameless doings, she showed a kindly interest in his, and on wet days condoled with him.

On the thirtieth of the month, a Friday, it rained so remorselessly that if he had not been tied to a Valuation for Probate he would have stayed in the shop. When he returned, nerved against condolences, he found himself welcomed back with the airs of a mama disclosing a surprise cake. "Look what's come in!"

It stood upended in the middle of the room, cylindrical as a length of earthenware drainpipe—which, in fact, it was—and gay as a Joseph's coat of many colors. The drainpipe having been plastered with some sort of bitumen, a medley of broken china and pottery had been pavemented all over it. The labor and ingenuity expended must have been prodigious; the aim, he supposed, to enrich a home with an ornamental umbrella stand. In short, a labor of love.

"English mosaic," remarked Miss Know-All Hartley. "Isn't it a marvelous specimen? I've never seen a better one."

After a first glance, Mr. Edom began to circle round the object with an expression in which reprobation deepened into woe.

"I don't wonder you're spellbound. I've been hanging over it all the afternoon. Have you noticed the bird's head sticking coyly out from the teapot handle?"

"Yes. It's Chelsea."

In the extremity of his anguish, he went down on his knees and peered into the medley. "That's Nantgarw," he moaned. "That's second-period Dr. Wall. That's Coalport. That's a Billingsley rose. That's Whieldon tortoise shell . . . and there's another bit of it . . . and another . . . and another! She must have had a whole dish and taken a hammer to it."

"How perfectly appalling! The ignoramus! But why are you so sure it was a woman?"

He did not reply. He had just found more of the Dr. Wall—judging by contours, a punch bowl. Still on his knees, he circled round the drainpipe, tracing, scrutinizing, identifying; and becoming increasingly sure that not only had a Whieldon dish and a Dr. Wall punch bowl been immolated on the altar of Home Art but also a

Nantgarw plate, a Cookworthy jug, and, almost certainly, a dozen Bristol teacups, since, in the compiler's enthusiasm for Billingsley roses, nine had been hacked out, and the remaining three, no doubt, broken past using. Insult had been added to outrage, for bits of kitchenware, alehouse mugs, simpering Victorian pomade pots jostled the fine porcelain, higgledy-piggledy. And as he shuffled round and round, the Chelsea bird, clasped in the half hoop of a broken kitchen-teapot handle, recurrently looked him in the eye with a disgraced facetiousness.

"But why are you so sure it was a woman?" she repeated.

"I'd expect it to be," he replied, not very attentively, since at that moment he had noticed a Felix Pratt tree upside down.

At length he rose and dusted the knees of his trousers. It was a tragedy, an act of blasphemy, a monument of busybody spoliation —but there was nothing to be done about it.

"Some inheriting lady's maid," he added. "Some clever Jael with a hammer. Snipping up brocade for kettleholders, pasting color plates into scrap albums...it's all the same, it's all woman's work!"

It was then (though in his state of stupor he did not accept the evidence of his eyesight until some ten minutes later) that he glanced up and saw what was in Miss Hartley's mind. Her gaze was traveling over the shelves, here resting, there disregarding. At intervals it returned to the drainpipe and dwelled on it; and while her gaze dwelled on the drainpipe, she smugly, dreamily, purposefully smiled. She had very long coarse eyelashes; when she blinked, they seemed to be whispering together.

His attention was called back to business when a woman who had been looking intently at something in the window came in, saying in an Australian accent, "I'd like to see that piece of Belleek. I collect Belleek." It was one of those love matches, occurring between improbable partners, that even the most experienced antique dealers could not foresee. He would never have expected this lady to collect Belleek; a string of racehorses would have seemed more likely. Meanwhile, Miss Hartley had retreated to the back of the shop, as was expected of her. The woman left, and he entered the purchase in his ledger. His mind returned to its state of woe. All those beautiful pieces—rarities, objects of unrepeatable perfection, unsurmisable value, but above all, so beautiful—broken to fragments and plastered hideously on a drainpipe...How could people do such things?

How could people do such things? Then he remembered the look on Miss Hartley's face, and how her glance had traveled, and rested, and traveled again; and what it had recurrently dwelled on. He heard his own fatal voice saying, "Woman's work." He could not have been more instrumental if he had put the hammer into her hand.

Never, Mr. Edom had confided in those happier days when he had an assistant fit to be confided in, never forget yourself and begin cherishing. When a dealer has taken all proper precautions, the obligation toward his stock in trade is at an end. If he begins cherishing, he exchanges the detachment of those who sell antiques for the torments of those who collect them. Every night will be charged with fire, flood, housebreakers, and acts of God. Every lorry going down the street will be headed for his windows. All persons who enter his shop will do so as potential destroyers—oafs who stub out cigarettes in Sheraton inlay, epileptics whose fits hurl them through a Chinese screen. His oldest, most esteemed customers will become swine bearing away pearls, while as for children—King Herod was a Dr. Barnardo compared with how he will feel about children. In short, if he is going to begin cherishing, he might as well become a mother and have done with it. But now maternity in its extremest form had seized on Mr. Edom. The wrongs done to that defenseless English china had exposed his sensibility, which, since the china had never been his to sell, was unarmored by professional detachment. Then onto the surface of this pure and abstract grief had crashed the image of Miss Hartley's hammer, poised above his own wares—the Pinxton "estate" dessert service, each piece painted with a different view of a gentlemen's park; the Meissen laundress, with her turned-up nose and delicately reddened elbows; the pair of Derby vases and the Nymphenburg cat. If he had refrained from cherishing them before, he made up for it now.

He must...He would...His thoughts rushed scrabbling from one expedient to another. He must get her out of the place, instantly. That was imperative. But on what pretext? One can't, in these organized days, say to a young woman "Go!" and be sure she will comply. She might raise objections, stand on her rights. And if she didn't, and went, she would go as a raging Fury and as a raging Fury return. No! The obvious, sensible thing to do, the thing everyone does in such cases, was to call in the police. A strong plainclothes policeman, stationed in the shop...But in these intellectualized days, police are not the docile public servants they used to be. They form theories, they want to get to the bottom of it, they know all about perversions, fixations, and complexes. If he were to say to a policeman, "I suspect she steals," since she demonstrably wasn't stealing he would lay himself open to a charge of slander. If he said, "She means to break my best china and stick it on a drainpipe," the policeman with the evidential drainpipe before his eyes would know a fixation when he saw one, would know that what was required was not a policeman but an alienist. Besides, a strong plainclothes policeman, strolling among the Galleries' antiques as though among wedding presents, would have a ruinous effect on business—quite apart from breakages.

A number of clocks, striking more or less at the same time, because Mr. Edom made a point of keeping his clocks in working order, announced that it was six.

"Well, Miss Hartley, closing time again. What an evening! I hope you brought your mackintosh." They were the first words he had spoken to her since his discovery of her intentions, and they sounded remarkably false.

"Always prepared, Mr. Edom." She put it on. She took up her handbag, in which she would conceal the hammer. "Shall I set the alarm?"

So she meant to come back that very night, did she? "No, don't trouble. I shall be staying a little longer. I'll see to it when I leave. Good night, Miss Hartley."

"Good night, Mr. Edom. Oh, by the way." She turned back. "The person who brought the English mosaic—called Turnbull—will be coming in about midday tomorrow."

She had blushed. For all her effrontery, with that "by the way" which preluded the person who had brought the English mosaic, she had blushed; the consciousness of her vile purpose had reddened her face.

"I'll be here."

If the person called Turnbull had been coming in a little before sunrise, Mr. Edom would have been there—on guard. When Miss Hartley's footsteps had died out, Mr. Edom rang up his housekeeper, saying that there was such a press of business that he proposed to work all night. He would be much obliged if she would bring him some sandwiches, a bottle of his usual claret, his razor, and a large thermos of black coffee. She was to come in a taxi. She came, having on her own initiative added a traveling rug, a clean shirt, a toothbrush, and, in addition to the grouse sandwiches for his supper, some egg sandwiches, in case he felt like making an early breakfast. She offered no comment on his intention of working all night, and this allayed any lurking notion that he might be behaving a little oddly. He settled himself in his private room, shaded the reading lamp so that no chink of light should disclose his presence, and switched on the electric fire. As he uncorked the claret, he realized that he was quite fervently hoping that Miss Hartley would not break in on his seclusion. If she did—well, he would be ready for her. Meanwhile, here was the *Decline and Fall*—a handsome edition in nine volumes, bound in tree calf, with the bookplate of someone called Humphrey Tilbury. Mr. Edom had kept it in his private room for years, going on with it at intervals.

The clocks striking one alarmed him by their brevity. More time had gone by than he had realized. Perhaps at this moment Miss Hartley was rolling her drainpipe through the silent streets. He sat up a little straighter and lit a cigarette. It was really quite absurd to suppose that she would break in, bringing a drainpipe. His brain must have been heated for such an idea to be entertained for a moment. Besides, she would also need bitumen—not an easy stuff to come by after closing hours. She would just come with a hammer. She might not even come with a hammer; she could come with a sack... The smooth, plump, calming hand of Edward Gibbon was already laid on Mr. Edom's brow. He read on, page after page. He began to take a rational view, to reject phantasmagorias, to put, with system, first things first. If Miss Hartley did not break in (and by 3:30 A.M. it had begun to seem unlikely that she was going to), she would reappear with her usual punctuality at nine-thirty. He would then, swiftly and surely, have to get rid of her—but as an employer, not as a murderer.

He would have to ask her to leave, and forthwith. For if he had to endure her for another day, he would be driven to violent means. "Miss Hartley, I must ask you to leave at once." Difficult words to speak out loud and bold. Inevitably, they would antagonize her; and that was the last thing he wished to do. For if she had really toyed with the vile intentions he had attributed to her (Gibbon was now well in the ascendant), antagonizing her would stir it all up again. He must have some pretext, something inoffensive and irrefutable. It was a pity he had finished the black coffee; it would have helped him to think. Byron could think on soda water, but Byron was an exceptional character. There was a decent remnant of claret, but he would need that for breakfast; even Byron (a hero to Mr. Edom) would not have concluded a night-long vigil by drinking soda water with egg sandwiches... There *must* be some pretext. Funerals are threadbare; one cannot plead a funeral. In any case, to say "Miss Hartley, I am going to a funeral; you must leave" would provoke the retort that his absence at a funeral would be the very reason she must remain to look after the shop; and in no time he would find himself departing for a mock funeral, leaving her alone to muse on grievance and revenge. Weddings, baptisms, the confirmation of a nephew were no better. Chimneys on fire...compulsive warnings in a dream...drains —No, drains would be fatal! Taking her out for the day—no real answer there. Exposure to smallpox—that might do. But suppose she was a Christian Scientist? As the light of dawn stole into the room, mental exhaustion compelled Mr. Edom to shave, to brush his teeth, to put on the clean shirt. This made him feel so much livelier that as he poured out his breakfast claret he broke into song:

> "Wine can clear
> The vapors of despair..."

et cetera. Wine and egg sandwiches—he saw with pleasure that there were a great many—would prompt him to a solution.

He was on the trail of a splendid solution when he fell asleep.

The burglar alarm went off. She had come, she was trying to break in! Stumbling to his senses, he realized that it was broad day, that she had come at her usual time, found the door locked, and was waiting outside.

"Good morning, Miss Hartley. I am so sorry to keep you on the doorstep. I somehow forgot to turn off the alarm. The fact is, a great deal has been happening since I saw you last. I have had to make a great many decisions. I find I must go to Constantinople. Yes, to Constantinople. At once. I can't go into it all; there isn't time. I don't know how long I shall be away, but it will be a matter of some weeks. So for the time being I am closing the Galleries. Which means, of course, that I shan't require your services any longer. I shall close the Galleries at midday, so you are free to go immediately, the moment I have made out your check. I shall include next week, of course, and your traveling expenses."

As he spoke, he watched her expression. It was one of frustration. There could be no doubt of her intentions, no doubt at all. Yet as he watched he saw her expression change. A sudden gleam, as though of relief, of renewed purpose, of complacency even, transformed her whole appearance. Good God, had she already thought of a way round?

The door had opened and a burly young man had come in. "Good morning," he said, addressing himself to Miss Hartley. "Hope I'm not too early. What's the verdict?" There was a burnish on his familiarity that suggested the familiarity was of recent date.

"No, Mr. Turnbull, never too early. Mr. Edom, this is Mr. Turnbull, who brought in the English mosaic."

"And a load and a half it was, too. It about did for the springs of my old bus. I hope I shan't have to take it away."

"It's an interesting piece," said Mr. Edom. "Of course, there's no market for English mosaic yet. One might say its hour has not yet struck. But it's an interesting piece. Is it a family possession?"

"Good Lord, no! No, I brought it here to oblige a friend. He was left it by a great-uncle, who set no end of store by it, because it was made by some ancestor or other. Quite a romantic story. His fiancée died."

"Indeed."

"Yes. The ancestor's, I mean. And he put up a monument to her in the garden. This was part of it—this and another like it, but that somehow got mislaid in a move. The rest of the monument was falling down by then. It must have been quite a lifework—stuck all over with fancy pebbles, and shells, and bits of colored glass, and his fiancée's name picked out in glass marbles: 'Eliza.' It's surprising what love will make a man do," he added, turning to Miss Hartley.

"Not nowadays," she said, and flicked her eyelashes at him.

"Wait till you know."

She bridled, and Mr. Turnbull increasingly smiled, and moved nearer.

Mr. Edom coughed. "As I was saying, it's an interesting piece. I wonder your friend doesn't want to keep it, since it has associations."

"Not he! He's a bit of a Socialist. Eliza and the Honorable Vavasour—did you ever hear such a name?—don't appeal to him. Nor any other bygones. He's modern. Now, I'm different." Again he turned to Miss Hartley. "I rather like a genuine antique. They've got something."

"Ten pounds," said Mr. Edom.

The enormity of such an offer distracted Miss Hartley from her own business to his. Incredulity, followed by contempt; contempt melting into gratification—she must have hated him intensely, to draw such pleasure from seeing him make a fool of himself.

"I should have thought it was worth more than that," said Mr. Turnbull.

"No—but I'll make it guineas, as I'm buying it as a present. For you, Miss Hartley," said Mr. Edom, bowing. "A parting present, a little souvenir. I'm sure you'll find it interesting."

Struggling with convulsive yawns, he tried to seem attentive to Miss Hartley's inattentive thanks and her hopes he would enjoy himself in Constantinople.

"Yes," concurred Mr. Edom. "Constantinople. I believe it is a very interesting city. Very historical. Would you like me to have your mosaic sent up to London after you?"

Mr. Turnbull, who had finished putting away his ten guineas, now looked up alertly. "What, are you going to London? Why don't I drive you? I was thinking of going there myself—as it happens."

"You'll have to wait while I pack, you know," said Miss Hartley.

"That's all right by me. I've got nothing special to do. I don't mind when I start."

With these gracious words, Mr. Turnbull shouldered the drainpipe. Miss Hartley followed him. Mr. Edom held open the door. They drove off, Mr. Turnbull rather flushed, Miss Hartley lofty and urbane, waving her hand in farewell. They took with them the bright relics of a forgotten craftsmanship, a vanished elegance, a very different outlook on love.

The Candles

IT WAS weather to be expected in January. The wind had backed from southerly to due east, turning the drizzling rain to sleet, then to snow. During the morning, only three people visited the Abbey Antique Galleries. Two came, hopefully but vainly, to try to sell Christmas presents they didn't want. The third was a dealer, who eventually decided not to buy a Sheffield candelabrum. All three quoted the proverb that as the days lengthen, the cold strengthens, and observed that there were a lot of colds about. Mr. Edom said to his assistant, Mr. Collins, whom he now from ripening esteem as often as not addressed as George, that they might as well shut up and go home for the afternoon. Mr. Collins thought not. His turn of mind inclined him to believe that it is darkest before dawn and that it was out of a snowstorm that some stranger was likeliest to walk in with a musical snuffbox. The lid would fly open, the tiny bird would open its beak, fill the air with a brief ecstasy of song, and vanish again, the lid falling after it with a faultless snap; the stranger would remark that his great-aunt had had quite a lot of such oddities—he set no store by them himself. Mr. Collins did not go into all this, but got his way by saying submissively that, if Mr. Edom did not object, he himself would come back in the afternoon, just in case. Mr. Edom then said very well, but in that case they would close from one to two, and George must come and lunch with him at the Abbey Grill.

The force of the wind hurried them down the street under a darkening sky. More snow was imminent. Before they had finished their meal, people were crowding in, badged with snow and talking in loud voices, as people do who come indoors after contending with rough weather. Mr. Edom said they would wait for the worst to go over, and ordered two glasses of port.

Against the wind, they struggled back through a scene that was unrecognizably hushed, unrecognizably noisy. One or two cars with their headlights on groped by; others were at a standstill. The air resounded with rattles and jangles and the screeching of overhead wires. They entered the shop, and it was as if they had never felt warmth before. When Mr. Edom had recovered his breath, he said conversationally, "Well, that was quite disagreeable." This came out pretty much as he intended, but even so, his teeth chattered and he felt an inclination to hold on to the nearest solid piece of furniture. Mr. Collins stood by the door and dripped.

There were times—this was one of them—when Mr. Edom could have wished his assistant hadn't got such long legs. When long legs are not actively engaged, they give an impression of standing about—which doesn't do. Still less does it do if they attract attention by rushing about on impulses of helpfulness and good will. In the antique trade, one should aim at being functional: an existence aloofly yet watchfully there, ready to come forward if required, meanwhile in reserve, partially obscured by a *bonheur-du-jour*, perhaps, or looking out of the window; but always unobtrusive as an angler, with legs fading into the landscape until called for, and with good will—if that article cannot be discarded—directed impersonally toward men but never to particular customers. Customers don't like good will; it makes them feel inferior. Similarly, it does not do to look pleased when something has been sold. It is for the customer to look pleased; the vender's part is to acquiesce—as with cheeks and kisses. But for all that, George, smiling like a Cheshire cat and with his good will constantly needing to be checked with a "Down, Ponto!," was no fool; and when it came to handling things he was as deft and reliable as a retriever dog.

While these thoughts were going through his mind, Mr. Edom, though he did not know it, was also smiling—not because of the mitigating merits of his assistant but because his feet were beginning to get warm. They seemed to be doing so at a distance and independently of him, but the development pleased him—as though they were beings far removed and no real relations of his, yet he felt a disinterested satisfaction at their well-being.

"Beginning to thaw, George?" he inquired.

Before Mr. Collins could reply, the lights went out. In the houses opposite, the lights had also gone out. Only the two electric fires retained a fading glare. While Mr. Edom was still finding words to say what he thought of the Electricity Board, Mr. Collins struggled into his wet overcoat and rushed from the shop.

Mr. Edom wrapped himself in a tigerskin and sat down in the bergère to conserve his vital heat—what there was of it. The glow faded from his feet as it had done from the two electric heaters. He wished he had not decided against oil heating. He wished his assistant had not gone mad. Dementia seemed a kinder supposition than heartless desertion: one should not think the worst of a man until one is categorically forced to. The room seemed to congeal about him like black ice. The wind kept up a steady screech. Looking out of his darkened box at the darkened housefronts opposite, he watched the driven snow horizontally twirling past, like the ghost of an unending rope. He rearranged the tigerskin, which was a poor fit. It was all very well to be charitable and suppose that Collins had gone mad, but it couldn't stop there: madness involves more than charitable suppositions. Someone would have to bear witness as to when he went mad, and how, and if he had previously shown signs of doing so. As a first step, he would have to telephone the police. At the thought of squandering his last illusion of keeping warm, Mr. Edom groaned. He began to founder in the cold of the room, the black ice was closing over his head, when the room became immeasurably colder. Mr. Collins had come in. His expression was elated; he positively appeared to glow. (Madmen, Mr. Edom had read, are often insensible to extremes of heat or cold; they live by the raging of their blood.) Under each arm he held a parcel.

"Candles," he said. "I was just in time to get the last two packets at Gay's."

"Candles," repeated Mr. Edom, his voice sounding a little wan after all he'd been through. "Candles. What a good idea."

"The moment the light went off, I thought to myself, Now's the time to sell candlesticks!"

It was another of those impulses of good will. Except for that inrush of cold air, nothing was likely to come of it; if those who sat in darkness had candles, they would stick them in bottles rather than go out to buy candlesticks. But the deed was done, so, repressing a "Down, Ponto!," Mr. Edom said again, "What a good idea," and added that it was lucky Beales hadn't taken the candelabrum. By the light of one candle, two candles, they assembled seventeen candleholders of various kinds and values, stuck candles in, and lit

them. At first these were grouped together. The effect was dissatis-
fying, so they began to disperse them about the room, standing back
to judge the effect, having better ideas, trying experiments, giving a
rub-up here and there. All this took some time, and was animating;
and when everything was arranged to their joint satisfaction, and
two long-nosed candle scissors in their gadrooned trays laid ready
for use on the sofa table, they sat down and agreed how nice it all
looked, and what a pity it was people didn't sit oftener by candlelight—it was so restful. And if at that point Mr. Collins' imagined
customers had stormed in to buy candlesticks, they would have
been unwelcome.

For in the diffused candlelight, everything had become mysteriously beautiful and enriched. The polished surfaces reflected the little flames with an intensification of their various colors—amber in
satinwood, audit ale in mahogany, dragon's blood in tortoise shell.
Glass flashed, silver asserted its contours, a tapestry bloomed into
life. The depth of the room seemed to be asleep. The candlelight
was an acceptance of darkness; the hideous daylight beyond the
window was a blue dusk, the driven snow a flicker of mayflies. Mr.
Edom sat gazing at his assembled wares. For all his knowledge of
them, for all his connoisseurship, he had never realized their beauty
before, nor their quality of character. The candlelight had freed
them from being wares in an antique shop. They were back at home
in it; they basked in the light of their best days; they were possessions, serene inmates of a household. He has more feeling than I
give him credit for, thought Mr. Collins, studying his employer's
face and the candlelight's new reading of its wrinkles. They sat in
silence. At intervals, Mr. Collins would get up and trim a candle-
wick, just for the pleasure of doing so.

The door was opened. The candle flames streamed sideways; Mr.

Edom stiffened. But it was Major Barnard who came in, saying, "I don't want to disturb you, but may I come in for a bit? It looks so cozy from outside, and so uncommonly pretty. I don't know that I've ever seen your things looking so pretty before." And he sat down as a friend does, and presently snuffed the air with pleasure, and remarked how agreeable the smell of candle wax is, and that it was a pity people didn't use them more often. "Warm, too," he went on. "At least it seems warm to me. But perhaps that's just by contrast."

"Candles do give out heat," said Mr. Collins. "It can be quite noticeable." He broke off, but the other two waited for him to go on. "When I was a boy," he went on, "I was sent to live with my London uncle. My parents had quarreled, you see, and the home was broken up. We were all sent off to different relations—anyone who'd take us—and I went to this uncle, to mix in with my cousins. It was the Christmas holidays, and I thought it would be wonderful, to be in London with so much going on. But it wasn't. They lived in Lambeth, and there wasn't much going on in Lambeth. So I took to going out by myself. I used to go across the river, and look into Gamage's windows and think what I'd buy out of them. Or to Liverpool Street Station, and fancy what train I'd take to where. But this particular day—it was biting cold; I'll never forget the wind over Blackfriars Bridge—I hadn't the heart to go so far, so I went into a church. It had a lot of things to look at—carved wood and gilding and flowers in vases; it even had a grand piano. But what caught my eye was an iron stand with sockets for candles, and three or four candles burning, and a tray with dozens more, and a notice saying 'Candles Twopence.' Well, I could afford two. And I began to feel a bit warmer when they had got going. But by then the others were beginning to burn down. I knew you lit candles for dead souls—I was inclined to be religious then—"

"One is at that age," said Major Barnard.

"—so I set to and thought of every dead person I knew of, or had heard of; and in no time I had every one of those candles alight. It was glorious. As good as a coal fire."

"Not bad for fourpence," said Mr. Edom.

"Don't suppose the boy had any more money," said Major Barnard.

"Threepence halfpenny, and I put that in. In the new year I was fetched away by my grandmother in Belfast, and I didn't have a chance to go back till 1945. The church had been burned out—a Wren church, too. The roof was gone; it was all boarded up. But there was a collecting box for rebuilding, so I paid in the end."

Overcome by embarrassment, Mr. Collins got up and trimmed every candle. When he recovered himself, Mr. Edom and Major Barnard were telling each other when and where they had been coldest. Mr. Edom had also been coldest in his boyhood. Major Barnard had never really known what cold was till he was a young man and got caught in a blizzard on Schiehallion. "Where's that?" asked Mr. Collins, and was told it is in the Highlands. Mr. Edom nodded gravely. "Speaking for myself," he said, "I never go out for anything you might call a walk without taking a bar of chocolate with me. Which reminds me—"

Taking up a bedroom candlestick, he disappeared into his office and returned with a bottle of brandy. He put this down on the sofa table, selected three wineglasses—not from the Waterford set but from the next best—and filled them. "To our host," said Major Barnard.

"Good luck to him," said Mr. Collins. Mr. Edom bowed, and let a polite interval pass before he drank himself.

"All this is uncommonly pleasant," observed Major Barnard. "I really don't know when I've spent a more agreeable afternoon.

I suppose you would still call it afternoon, though from the look of things outside it might as well— What's that?"

That was a shape plastered to the windowpane. Black and shiny, with a pinched face and eyes reflecting the light within, it looked like some kind of portentously large bat. It was in fact a small boy in an oilskin cape too large for him.

"It's a boy," said Major Barnard. "We can't leave him outside, you know. Come in, boy."

Major Barnard was still under the influence of Mr. Collins' story, told in that flat cheap accent, with the echo of a child's lonely defiance still hanging about it, or he would not have made so free with his host's hospitality. His mind misgave him at the boy's first words, which were "Don't mind if I do." This was one of those alarming new children, born into a nuclear age and scornful of everything not potentially destructive.

"Why have you got those lights on, all over the place like that? Nobody else has."

"They're candles," Mr. Collins said. "Haven't you ever seen candles before?"

"No. Do they run off a battery?"

"They burn by themselves. With a wick, like an oil lamp; but instead of floating in oil the wick is fed by the wax melting round it." Mr. Collins saw his explanations quite disregarded. "Look," he said, proffering a candle. "Blow this one out, not too hard, just a puff, and I'll light it again." The boy drew back, compressing his lips. Mr. Collins blew out the candle and relit it.

"Do you have to do all that?" said the boy. "Matches, and all. Haven't you got a lighter?"

"Matches are tidier," said Mr. Edom. "If you use a lighter, it makes the wax run, and spoils the look of the candle."

"I don't see why that matters, if the wax melts anyway."

"I wouldn't suppose you did." Mr. Edom's voice was glassily urbane, and the boy instantly subsided. Major Barnard seized the advantage. "Why aren't you at home, boy? This is no weather to be out in."

"Going to visit my Gran. She's old-fashioned. She's got a coal fire." To cancel the disgracing admission, he went on, "And a canary bird. And a horn gramophone. And a hand sewing machine. And the works of William Shakespeare. And a cataract. And—Hi!" The electricity had come on. Everything looking as usual looked as if it had been flayed. "That's more like it!" shouted the boy. "No bloody Gran now!" He was off like a bird out of its cage.

Major Barnard, turning to Mr. Edom, said, "I'm sorry about that. Not a very nice boy."

"Ignorant," Mr. Edom replied.

Mr. Collins was going to and fro putting out the candles. A sweet smoke hung on the air and was like a sigh. He carried the candle-sticks to the back of the shop, removed the candles, laid them on a sheet of brown paper, and began to chip the cooling wax off the sconces with his nail.

"Leave them till tomorrow, George. We'll be off now. There's nothing to stay for," said Mr. Edom.

Major Barnard gathered up the tigerskin and smoothed it. "Where does this—"

The lighting staggered, and went off.

Major Barnard produced his pocket torch. By its beam Mr. Edom put the valuables away in the safe, locked his office desk, turned off the switches, set the alarm. They went out together, exclaiming at the depth of the snow. But the storm was over. Mr. Edom and his assistant went their ways, Major Barnard went his, thinking how pretty the candles had been, and of their warmth still gently dying in the darkness.

Furnivall's Hoopoe

WHEN Mrs. Otter came into the Abbey Antique Galleries that morning, Mr. Edom, the proprietor, saw with concern that her hat was straight, her hair tidy, her handbag clasped. Something must be very wrong.

"Oh, Mr. Edom, I am so thankful to get you to myself." She broke off, trying to recover her breath. "You know, it's my positive belief that St. John Street gets steeper every day. I should not be in the least surprised to find myself picking edelweiss there. Not that I like edelweiss; it's such a coldhearted flower, though it meant a great deal to our great-grandparents, plunging into crevasses to snatch it for their Louisas. I'm sure it can't be only my increasing years which make me so out of breath by the time I get here— though at the moment I am feeling dreadfully old."

She sat down, holding her bag upright on her knee like a person applying for a situation. Her glance strayed over the Dresden shepherd playing the flute to his dog, the pewter tankards on the mule chest, the Nailsea birds poised on their crystal branch, the wig stand, the three Portuguese reliquaries, the satinwood *bonheur-du-*

jour as though in one or other of these she might find reassurance. But nothing supplied it, and the glance returned to Mr. Edom and rested on him so disconsolately that he began to feel that he too must fail her.

"The trouble is, all your things are so beautiful, so tip-top. I've got nothing you could conceivably want."

Remembrance of past transactions with Mrs. Otter told him that this might well be true. At the far end of the room, the reflection of Mr. Collins' face, encompassed by the blue plaster bows of a rococo mirror, repeated the same tale, and in sterner accents. He had bought a great deal of rubbish from the dear lady. On the other hand, she had sometimes brought off a winner.

"Don't say that, Mrs. Otter. Have you forgotten those dueling pistols you found in the attic which Mrs. Vibart carried off for her collection? George sold her two of his kittens at the same time." This should settle George Collins.

"Yes, wasn't it glorious? But I have no more dueling pistols. Nothing but assegais and baby clothes."

And he'll buy them, thought Mr. Collins. Undoubtedly there must be something about Mrs. Otter, since Mr. Edom felt whatever it was so strongly. For himself, Mr. Collins felt nothing except a loyal resignation. He went on looking in a bible of china marks for TBZ, with "Patmos" in a crowned lozenge.

Mrs. Otter enlarged. "All the same, I think I'm going to ask you to come and look, just in case you should find something I've missed. You see, the pistol money went to my idiot boy to help buy an enormous Edwardian car because he wanted to drive to Brighton. Well, that was all right, and he was towed back, and when it was repaired he took it out to show to a friend who rather thought of buying it, which would have paid for the repairs, which had come to more than he expected, because apparently when you have an Edwardian car its inside bits are period pieces too. So he was on his way to the friend, who shares a flat in Chelsea, when he saw another friend who was marching in a peaceful demonstration or perhaps it was a counter-demonstration—anyway, it was peaceful—and the friend said join in, so Toby joined in, going as slow as he could and then waiting for them to catch up, and it gave new life to the demonstration, and whole busloads cheered, and everything was perfectly all right till they got to the Embassy; but by then the car had overheated from going so slow, and it skidded and rushed halfway up the Embassy steps. No one was hurt, but the Embassy people were very prim about it, and Toby was arrested; and as his license is endorsed up to the hilt he'll either have to pay a fine or go to prison. Personally, I would welcome a term in prison, prison sounds so calm. But the young don't want calm."

"It will be a pleasure," said Mr. Edom, putting his foot firmly on the further end of Mrs. Otter's statement. "I'll come at once, if that would be convenient."

"Perhaps not quite at once. I ought to do a little tidying first."

"Shall we say, this afternoon, at three?"

"At quarter to four. Then I can give you tea." She was already looking more like herself. Her hat had drifted to the back of her head and a ringlet had escaped and hung engagingly over her nose.

It is the doom of man to love what he is not constructed for. Mrs. Otter was too often tipsy. She dressed like a tinker, and if by chance she was driven into respectable new clothes she instantly got them into bad ways. Her reactions were incalculable. She combined being vague with being arbitrary. In terms of cabinetmaking, silverware, ceramics, Mr. Edom would never have admitted her into his Galleries. But from the hour he first set eyes on her (a horse had fallen down in St. John Street and she was sitting on its head), he had loved her against all his principles, and fatalistically, as fathers love. So—but without impediment of principles—did every errand boy, every street hawker, and all the town's crusted bad characters. He wasn't much among so many, and probably at their various times they had all had tea with her. But today it was his turn.

Her Lapsang soochong was exquisite, but he felt a traitor as he drank it. There was treachery in allowing her to foist such rubbish on him: alphabet mugs without handles, souvenirs from Jerusalem, that hatbox with associations (he had avoided it till now, but it had got him at last); worst of all, ruins of what had once been splendors. He was packing the sorry assortment in the hatbox when she remembered what it was she had been meaning to say ever since he arrived: Would he like a scrap screen?

The scrap screen was in her bedroom. Its eight-fold span glorified half a wall with the colors of a hothouse, the richness of a plum pudding, the glow and multiplicity of the Last Judgment window in the Minster. And even to his trained and anxious eye it seemed in quite remarkably good condition. Mistaking his silence, she said propitiatingly, "It's done on the other side too. But it's not so lively, as by then they had to fall back on engravings."

"Who were 'they,' Mrs. Otter?"

"My first husband's great-aunts. Eight of them, and each did a leaf. They lived in a rectory in north Norfolk and were always in quarantine for something or other. Would you like to see the other side?"

He answered that he would take the other side on trust and send packers and a van in the morning. Meanwhile, he would put a check in the post—a provisional check—for he hoped to do considerably better.

He was so elated by the prospect of enriching Mrs. Otter that not till he was on the threshold of the Galleries and saw Mr. Collins at the telephone did he remember that he did not go in for large Victoriana.

"That was Mr. Grimshaw," said Mr. Collins, putting back the receiver.

"Domes, I suppose?" Mr. Grimshaw was the curator of the stuffed birds in the town museum.

"I told him you had no unoccupied domes, but he saw the dome of the Nailsea birds through the window, and he's coming tomorrow to measure it and make an offer."

"He can offer," said Mr. Edom.

"And Mrs. Harington may be coming too. She wants to try if the harp stool is comfortable."

"Quite a party."

"Why, who else?"

"Mrs. Otter's scrap screen. We must think about placing it. It's six foot high, and to be seen to advantage it will need twelve-foot-by-four-foot floor space."

Forty minutes later Mr. Collins, putting on his coat again, remarked that Mr. Edom ought to have been a general.

The van came punctually next morning. Mrs. Otter came too, sitting beside the driver and holding the hatbox. The screen was carried in. Freed from its wrappings and expanded in its resting place, it looked imposingly spectacular and totally out of keeping with its surroundings. But Mr. Grimshaw, single-hearted in his devotion to British birds and their post-mortem preservation, walked in without paying it the slightest attention.

"I've come about that dome. But I don't see it, though it was here yesterday. You seem to have moved everything. What's the object— Oh, there it is." He produced his pocket rule and made careful, censorious measurements. "It's a bit cramped, but it will have to do. I'll take it. I must say, I wonder what in God's name these flimflam objects were meant for? How could any bird fly with wings like ballet girls' skirts, I'd like to know."

"You will take the group?"

"The group? Good God, no! It's the dome I want."

Mrs. Harington had now come in, carrying an opossum muff. Leaving Mr. Collins to explain to Mr. Grimshaw that the dome could not be sold without its denizens (a routine matter but wrongheadedness sprang eternal in Mr. Grimshaw), Mr. Edom went to greet her. He was too late. She had gone straight to the screen and had eyes for nothing else. She was always lovely, but never before had he seen her look like this: enfranchised by pleasure at the brilliant paper mosaic.

"And there's so much of it!" she exclaimed.

Her intent gaze traveled from seedsman's-catalogue carrots to giraffes, copper kettles, smirking blond children in pinafores, Grace Darling, marrow-fat peas, Indian braves, Goody Two-shoes, the Taj Mahal, dahlias, chest expanders, guardian angels, trophies of grapes, peaches and nectarines, foxhunters, cauliflowers, steam engines, illuminated texts, gorillas, Persian kittens, hip baths, crocodiles, robins, General Gordon, Eno's Fruit Salts, camellias, pineapples, sewing machines—their irrefutable fortuity firmly pasted on and guarded by the splendid varnish of the period. The traveling gaze reached the edge of the screen, flicked inattentively over the shabby human figure standing by it, went back to the solemn raptures of discovery. Mr. Edom stole a congratulatory glance at Mrs.

Otter—and realized that in another moment she would be giving the screen away.

"Mrs. Harington, do you know Mrs. Otter? We are selling the screen for her."

"How do you do? I'm afraid I've been rude, thinking of nothing but your screen. Please forgive me and tell me about it. What's this queer thing, next to the lobster?"

"A mangle, for squeezing wet washing in before you hang it on the line."

"What a good idea! And this?"

"A bonnet."

Their voices mingled. Of the two voices, Mrs. Otter's sounded the younger. Presently, they were down on their knees, studying the base of the screen.

"The bull, Mrs. Otter! Look at the bull!"

Below the bull a hand in the Norfolk rectory had stuck an illuminated text: *He shall be called Wonderful.*

"Do you think it was his real name? It's the sort of name people give bulls. Or was it a coincidence?"

"I wish I knew. I've often wondered about it." Mrs. Otter was stroking the opossum muff.

Meanwhile Mr. Grimshaw, who had paused before a small ivory Annunciation to comment injuriously on the angel's deficiency in pectoral muscles—how did Mr. Collins suppose it would ever get off the ground again?—was slowly making his way out from behind the screen. An engraving caught his eye. As if the bull called Wonderful had materialized, a strangled yell rang through the Galleries.

"Furnivall's hoopoe! Furnivall's hoopoe! I say, Edom, do you know you've got a Furnivall's hoopoe here?"

"And begonias!" murmured Mrs. Harington.

"Jammed in among all these tomfool foreign cathedrals. It's a marvel I saw it. Furnivall's hoopoe, by Wilkins. What a find—and I daresay you hadn't even noticed it. Do you know, the last Furnivall's hoopoe in this country was shot in 1852? By a clergyman, needless to say. Pity nobody shoots clergymen."

Mr. Edom made a deprecatory noise.

"I tell you, the Church of England has wiped out ninety percent of the rare birds in this country. All those country parsons, they all had guns, they all fancied themselves as naturalists, they all had six days of the week to do nothing in. So whenever they saw a rare bird, they shot it. Go into any ornithological museum and read the tickets. Shot by the Reverend Mr. So-and-So. Shot by the Reverend Mr. So-and-So. What a pack!"

Mrs. Otter from her side of the screen took up the challenge. "Fiddlesticks, Mr. Grimshaw. Both my husbands were Church of England clergymen and neither of them shot as much as a canary."

"Why should they? Canaries are as common as sparrows. They left canaries to their wives and went out to extirpate siskins and choughs and avocets and rare migrants like Furnivall's hoopoe. It makes my blood boil."

"And the stuffed birds in the museum," retorted Mrs. Otter, "those which weren't shot by clergymen. Do you suppose they all died a natural death?"

"Madam, you stray from the point. The purpose of an ornithological museum—"

"Ornithological shrike's larder," interposed Mrs. Otter.

"If you are referring to *Lanius collurio*, I will admit that I hold no brief for the bird, but—"

"*I* do. At least shrikes have the decency to eat what they've killed, which is more than ornithologists do."

While the contest raged from either side of the screen and a customer came in only to say she would be calling later and hurry out, Mrs. Harington went on enumerating toads, volcanoes, turkeys, etc. Maddened by this incessant cooing, harassed by Mrs. Otter's agility in straying from the point, Mr. Grimshaw broke off and went back to his first purpose. "Edom. I will take the engraving of Furnivall's hoopoe. How much do you want for it?"

Mrs. Harington sprang to her feet. "If you think you are going to have my screen—"

"There, there, don't get excited. Of course he shan't" and "I understand the screen is already under offer," said Mrs. Otter and Mr. Edom, speaking simultaneously.

"Nothing would induce me to buy it," said Mr. Grimshaw. "All I need is the engraving of Furnivall's hoopoe. I presume it can be peeled off."

"I doubt it. I very much doubt it," said Mr. Edom. "Mid-nineteenth-century paste is very tenacious."

"And as it happens, I want Furnivall's hoopoe too," Mrs. Harington declared. "I'm very fond of hoopoes."

Mr. Grimshaw's sardonic laughter behind the screen sounded quite devilish. The screen itself trembled. The tip of a penknife appeared in the center of Grace Darling.

"You old beast, you sneaking old beast!" exclaimed Mrs. Harington; and with great force and accuracy she hurled the opossum muff over the screen in a line with Grace Darling. There was the sound of a strong man struggling with a mouthful of fur. The penknife made another slash.

Mr. Edom said, "George."

Mr. Collins stepped forward, and inexpressively, like a force of nature, conveyed Mr. Grimshaw into the street.

Saying, "You were marvelous," Mrs. Harington threw herself into Mrs. Otter's arms.

"So were you," replied Mrs. Otter. "Avenging and bright. Now shall we all sit down? Do sit down, Mr. Collins."

Mr. Collins sat down and smoothed the muff, which Mr. Grimshaw had used as a boxing glove. Mrs. Otter advised him to pretend he was in the Salvation Army and give it a good shake. He did so.

There was a long silence spent in getting over it. Mrs. Harington was the first to speak.

"Now I must buy it, mustn't I? What's so extremely grand is that I can. Richard gave me a hundred pounds yesterday, to buy myself a present. Will that be enough?" Before Mrs. Otter could get her word in, Mr. Edom said, "It would have been handsome, Mrs. Harington, but now it's excessive. The screen is no longer in mint condition. I think it can be repaired, but I can't in conscience ask more than ninety. George. Did you happen to notice what it's like at the back?"

"The bird's all right. He took care of that. But the Tower of London's a bit knocked about."

The two men went off to consider the damage. Mrs. Harington moved closer to Mrs. Otter. "I wonder if I ought to give him his bird. I'm afraid he was rather set on it."

"It would be a kind thing to do—if you could manage it without putting his back up."

"I wasn't thinking of being kind. I was thinking about being on the safe side. For suppose he decided to steal it? Suppose I woke up one night and heard the magnolia creaking and saw his face glaring in at my bedroom window and it came out on the baby as a port-wine hoopoe."

"If I were you, I wouldn't give it another thought. For one thing, he's respectable at heart and would never climb up someone else's magnolia. For another, speaking as an experienced matron, all this talk about birthmarks is bugaboo."

Mrs. Harington opened her lovely mouth, then closed it again. When the screen had been settled, the two ladies left together, as Mrs. Otter was being given a lift home. Mr. Edom watched their departure with satisfaction. It had all turned out very nicely: Toby Otter would not go to prison and his mother would be left with a comfortable remainder. Yet it seemed to him that despite this happy ending a sudden cloud had shadowed her, a resignation, a tremor of regret for something precious and irrecoverable, not to do with the screen.

The Listening Woman

IT IS common experience how the possessions of one's childhood vanish: the blue and white mug with D on it, picturing a dog and a duck and a dairymaid, and at the bottom when you have drunk up your milk, a daisy; the *ombres chinoises* marionettes, with strings attached to their joints—and if you pulled injudiciously, their elbows started up level with their ears, while their faces retained an impassive scornfulness for such mere contortions; the stuffed printed-cotton cat, on whose oval base were four mushroom-colored underpaws, a triumph of art and realism; the high chair, detestable because it was childish, but with a better side to its character since it raised you to the level whence you could see out of the window; the picture of Queen Victoria, and the watercolor landscape with the moon and the row of silhouetted fir trees that you privately connected with wolves and weren't easy about; and the carved wooden bear brought from Switzerland, and the red velvet pincushion, and the dolls' dinner service—all scattered, all gone, broken or left behind in house moving or given away. All gone from your ungrateful memory, too, forgotten for half a century or only brought to mind by something in a display cabinet; having emerged from neglect and oblivion as an antique, rare and costing a great deal of money.

And then, suddenly, when you are an old woman—though not in your case a rare and valued antique—they flock back; and as they reappear you discover that they are far more yours than you supposed—that you remember everything about them, the crack that ran through the dairymaid, the smell of the bear and of the pincushion, the rattle of the dolls' soup tureen because the lid didn't quite fit, the mild supportingness of the cat when used as a pillow. They are more faithful than you.

Mr. Collins, the assistant at the Abbey Antique Galleries, did not interrupt this train of thought that a thimble case had aroused in the old lady's mind. She was a Miss Mainwaring, and said by his employer, Mr. Edom, to be knowledgeable—high praise on those controlled lips. Mr. Edom did not acclaim this quality often—perhaps once a year or so. She was an aunt of Canon Balsam's, and visited. During those visits she would come to have a look round the Galleries, and this was what she was doing now. It was the first time Mr. Collins had been tête-à-tête with her; but her presence was so contained and her examination so unobtrusive—she was not one of those people who take things up or ask to have things taken down —that to all intents and purposes he might have been alone. Ultimately, she would buy something—if only for manners' sake. She was one of the old lot.

Mr. Edom was out, doing a valuation. That same morning he had come back from the auction rooms with a tea chest full of pewter —measures, platters, tankards, and tobacco boxes, collected by the late Randolph Fyffe-Randolph, M.F.H.—remarking that a good half of it was Britannia metal but the remainder not too bad. Mr. Collins was now peering into the remainder for touch marks. Touch marks are the devil, for pewterers had no conscience and stamped them here, there, and anywhere. He had settled a tankard—William Tomkins—and was thankfully putting it by when he happened to glance inside the lid. There, near the rim, was a different set of touch marks. He checked the second set of marks. If the lys was in fact a scepter and the mark like B face downward an elephant, the lid was David Oliphant, Anne and George I. A lid might have been wrenched off and replaced by an earlier lid; but the hinge showed no sign of this and the tankard, now that he came to look at it as a piece of pewter and not merely a field for touch marks, seemed a cut above William Tomkins, who supplied mostly pothouse stuff under George III. If William Tomkins had bought the tankard in a job lot —as he might well have done if he was short of stock just then—a begrimed David Oliphant tankard might have been handed to an apprentice for a rub-up, and the apprentice tempted to illicit sporting with the punches. Or was this being imaginative? Mr. Collins glanced at Miss Mainwaring and wondered if she was knowledgeable about pewter.

He saw her halt in front of a carved and gilded oblong frame. She was knowledgeable about frames, anyhow. He saw her look with a tranquil smile at the blackened oil painting on wood. He heard her say, "So here you are."

The candlelit woman leaning from the window was no darker than she had always been. If you were acquainted with her, you could distinguish the rim of her linen cap against the hooding shadow behind, and the hand holding the candlestick, and the other hand shielding the flame—the flame whose light shone gently and ruddily on the oval face, coloring the nearer cheek and the tip of the long nose and laying areas of shadow between the cheekbones and the rather small almond-shaped eyes. There she was. No restorer, no flaying turpentined hand, had come between them. Unchanged, she was still watching from her window, unalarmed, patient, and slightly amused; still, after more than half a century, waiting for Lucy Mainwaring to come into her grandfather's library.

She had watched several generations of Mainwarings. Grandfather's grandfather, a squire in Cambridgeshire, had taken her in quittance of a debt, together with a Watteau that turned out to be a Pater. They hung on either side of the fireplace, being much the same size. For a while the Watteau that turned out to be a Pater had been Lucy's preference: you could see more of it, and the lady had a lap dog. You could see more of it, and that was why after a year or two you saw there wasn't much in it. The lady sat propped against the balustrade like a doll, and the legs of the gentleman playing the mandolin were not a pair. But the other one, the older you grew and the oftener you looked at it, the more there was to see, to see into, to think about. So it came to be called Lucy's picture.

Time sweeps one on, sweeps one into the enthusiasms of one's adolescence and out of them into fresh enthusiasms. Lucy was sixteen and living for Botticelli when her grandfather died. The house was sold, the property distributed. Aunt Lalage, who lectured about Anglo-Saxons at Girton, went off with the library books, and with the books went the two pictures. Mother resented this. It was such a beautiful old frame; Lalage had no appreciation of antiques and would probably stick a fancy portrait of Beowulf in it—the last thing in the world Grandfather had intended. And whenever she and Lalage met—which was seldom—she would ask, "Have you still got Lucy's picture?" Lucy saw her picture once or twice on Lalage's wall. No, noted it: she did not see it. By then she was living for D'Annunzio, and for a young man called Dennis Macnamara, who thought all that sort of thing great rot and died of dysentery in Mesopotamia. Lucy remained a spinster. Aunt Lalage maturely married a don, who was Welsh and made everyone read the Mabinogion. They retired to the land of his fathers and Lucy's picture was lost in the mists of Snowdonia.

But here it was.

Mr. Collins had heard her quiet exclamation. Obviously it had not been addressed to him, since here he already was. But when a lady speaks, especially such an old lady, it is manners to get up. He got up. Having got up, he realized that it would not be manners to sit down again. Mr. Edom had a particular way of approaching contemplative customers that Mr. Collins in his clandestine heart called the Funeral Gondola. It was inimitable, though no doubt part of it came by practice. Mr. Collins practiced a few hushed strokes forward, and the old lady turned to him and said, "I recognized it."

If she could do that through all those layers of varnish, she was certainly knowledgeable about the Dutch Masters.

"A Schalcken," he said.

She nodded.

"The frame is unusually fine," he continued. "It is contemporary. It was probably made for that very picture."

"So I have always understood," said the old lady. "You see, it's my picture." She turned back to the Schalcken and smiled at it.

Poor old thing, she must be a little mad. He must deal with her gently—but he wished Mr. Edom would come back.

When people get up on your account, it is never easy to get them down again. Lucy Mainwaring also wished that Mr. Edom would come back, and faithful Ponto, his watchdog, return to those tankards. Instead, here he was, lankly hovering. She would have to say something to him. What a pity, when she had so much to say to the woman leaning out of the window; or rather, so much to ask, for she herself had not very much to tell.

"Where did Mr. Edom get her?"

Mr. Collins did the best he could, which was to pretend he hadn't heard. For this was appalling—at any rate it was on the brink of becoming appalling. The poor old thing wasn't going to stop at being a little mad. She was going to work herself up, *idée fixe*, persecution mania, and all that. How on earth was he to deal gently with an elderly maniac, convinced that the Schalcken was her picture and had been stolen from her? He looked to see if she had an umbrella. She hadn't; but she could do a lot of execution with that handbag. If force of godless prayer could have fetched Mr. Edom back, Mr. Edom would have darkened the door at that same instant. Instead, it was a couple inflamed by a television series about adventures in finding unidentified antiques. Mr. Collins knew that kind at a glance—perhaps because there, but for the grace of God, he might have been adventuring himself.

"I don't suppose you've got any old books," said the lady.

So they were on the prowl for edge-paintings, were they? Mr. Collins had no patience with this craze for edge-paintings. He liked a handsome binding as well as any man; but with the spine of a book, and its sides, not to mention its interior, to be decorative on, tricking out its fore-edge—where at most a decent gilding should prevail—with esoteric views of St. Paul's or what not, was going too far.

He indicated a row of Surtees, a broken set of Migne's *Patrologiae*, Hakluyt's *Navigations*, and Bewick's *Birds*. They took up each volume in turn, held it slantingly frontwise to the light, and spun the pages. "I'm afraid none of these are quite what we want," said the man. "Do you go in for Art Nouveau?" And the woman said, "Have you any old Victorian jewelry?"

They were not nice people, but they were providential. Relieved of the necessity of throwing sticks for Mr. Edom's Ponto, Miss Mainwaring went on interrogating the woman at the window. Here she was—but how had she got here? Through what dusty auction rooms, unsurmisable ownerships, perils? Lalage had died in 1942, with a small obituary in the *Times*. Her don survived her by six years, so earning a rather larger obituary, as by then there was more room for civilian demises. Nineteen years, then, had been spent by the candlelit lady in traveling from Merionethshire to Oxfordshire. But she might well have been blown out of her course. One of the unsurmisable owners, a bank manager, say, or a clergyman, power-less as a Jesuit under authority, could have been directed to a wider usefulness at Wolverhampton, from Wolverhampton to Brighton. Considered in that light, she had been expeditious; though she looked composed as ever, she might even be rather out of breath, having got to the Abbey Antique Galleries only just in time.

"Well, what about pictures? What's that old picture over there, for instance?"

They stood on her heels and, being polite, she moved aside. Trusty Ponto followed them, looking as if he might snap at any moment.

"It's quite interesting," said the man. "What you can see of it. What's it supposed to be?"

"Dutch School," said Mr. Collins, his eye resting on Miss Mainwaring.

"Ah! One sees a lot of that. What do you think of it, Freda?"

"I'm not all that set on pictures, as you know. They take up such a lot of wall space."

"This one wouldn't. It's a kit-cat. I must admit, I don't mind it. I believe I rather like it. It would come up a lot with cleaning."

"I quite like the frame," said the lady.

"Yes, you're right. It's a very handsome frame—or would be, with a re-gilding."

"But I can't say I'm drawn to the picture—what you can see of it. It strikes me as monotonous. And it would cost the earth to clean."

"We could have a bash at the cleaning ourselves," said the man. "Enough to get some idea what it's like. And then, if we didn't care for it, we could always take it out and use the frame for something else. Why not?"

"Have it your own way," said the lady.

The man pulled out a notecase. "How much?" he said.

"One thousand five hundred guineas," said Mr. Collins.

"No, thank you!" exclaimed the lady.

The man, assuming dignity, said he would think it over, and added, "Come on, Freda. There's nothing here."

Blithely preceding them to the door, Mr. Collins saw that Mr. Edom was standing just inside it. How much he had heard and what he thought of it could not be deduced. But Mr. Collins did not feel the relief he had anticipated. He hoped to feel it later on—which is a different sensation. "Miss Mainwaring is here, Mr. Edom."

Mr. Edom had already recognized the small figure at the end of the room. It struck him that Miss Mainwaring had aged since her previous visit—had aged quite surprisingly. If this was to be her last visit to the Galleries it was distressing that it should have exposed her to customers like those who had just gone out. She turned as he approached. Her face was deathly white. Her lips twitched. She should not have been left standing about while those barbarians were ravaging the shop. He handed her a chair, and she sat down like one utterly exhausted.

"I always think these unexpected returns of summer so late in the autumn are very trying," Mr. Edom said. "One isn't prepared for them."

There was something else Mr. Edom wasn't prepared for, thought Mr. Collins. She was quiet enough now—for which he took some credit to himself, since you would need to be uncommonly far out of your wits for the sum of one thousand five hundred guineas not to come as a quietener; it got rid of that clever couple fast enough. But though she was quiet, she was working herself up. He could feel it in the air. In another minute Mr. Edom would be blown out of his Indian summers by the knowledgeable Miss Mainwaring claiming the Schalcken as her own property and demanding to know how he came by it. If only he'd been able to slip in a word of warning!

Sure enough, she was beginning again. "Mr. Edom, I want the Schalcken."

Mr. Edom said there was no one he would rather see it go to. It was a very nice little bit of genre. He'd taken a fancy to it the moment he set eyes on it.

"I saw it before you did, though. It belonged to my grandfather. I haven't seen it for fifty years or so, but I recognized it."

"That doesn't surprise me, Miss Mainwaring. If I may say so, you've got an eye."

"I've left it a little late. But I must have it. I loved it very much. It was always spoken of as Lucy's picture. I even thought it was really mine. And now, after all these years..."

Years of forgetfulness, faithlessness, contempt, she thought; and years of faithful abidingness. Meanwhile Mr. Edom, his heart unbuttoning to romance, was saying that journeys end in lovers' meeting.

Mr. Collins felt an oncome of second thoughts. Nothing could be less like madness than Miss Mainwaring's request for a book to write on, to save getting up. She laid the book on her knee, spread open the checkbook, and began to write, frowning a little when it came to reducing the guineas to pounds, shillings, and pence.

"There!"

Some dealers in their arrogance affect not to look at checks. Mr. Edom always looked carefully at his. He did so now, and looked yet again. He coughed. "Miss Mainwaring. I'm sorry, but you haven't made this out right."

"Oh! Haven't I? How stupid of me. Well, tell me the amount, and I'll alter it."

"I paid eighty-five pounds for that picture," said Mr. Edom. Mr. Collins, wrenched from his second thoughts by total amazement, could hardly believe his ears. No reputable dealer discloses what he paid for a thing. To do so is unethical, strikes at the root of society, and lowers the tone of the trade. Yet here was Mr. Edom, that model of decorum, blurting out his eighty-five pounds without a decency-bit of "in the region of," and continuing, "If you will pay me a hundred guineas, I shall have made my profit. And we will both be pleased, I hope."

Such is human vanity that for a moment Lucy Mainwaring was extremely angry that her grandfather's Schalcken should have been bought for eighty-five pounds. She made out another check, and Mr.

Edom receipted it. "But what I cannot understand," he exclaimed, "is how you got that other figure."

She saw Mr. Collins wishing the earth would swallow him up. "That man who left just as you came in was asking about it. I expect I misheard. I could easily have misheard. You see, I was so afraid he might get it." And seeing that Mr. Edom was not perfectly convinced, she added, "Now that she is mine, do tell me where you found her."

"I bought it from a publican in a village near Swindon. It was hanging in the snug."

She had an extraordinarily pretty laugh—a thing you don't often hear nowadays. But she was still looking white as a sheet, and her pretty laugh was like blossom on a winter bough. Having taken down the picture and set it on a level with Miss Mainwaring's view, Mr. Edom remarked, "As this is quite an occasion, I feel we should celebrate it." And going into his private room he returned with a bottle of hock and three glasses. "You too, Collins," he said, filling him the third glass. "And I suggest as a toast: All's well that ends well." His eye rested on Mr. Collins as he spoke, but blandly, and like an act of oblivion.

By the time Mr. Edom refilled her glass, Miss Mainwaring had begun to look more like herself. Still staring at the picture, she murmured, "I've made a discovery. I thought I knew everything about her, but I've made a discovery. She's not watching. She's listening." Mr. Edom took a careful scrutiny of the oval face. "Quite true. You're right, Miss Mainwaring. She's listening. Listening for a step she's waiting for, I should say."

"Come to that," added Mr. Collins, "you wouldn't see much on a dark night, holding a candle in front of your eyes like that. Schalcken liked his candlelight effects. But she's listening." For Mr.

Collins felt he could rejoin society. It was true that he had misstated the price, but he was not the only person who had been unprofessional about his figures that afternoon.

Yes, she was listening. She was listening for a step in the darkness, the step of someone nearing the end of a journey, or the step of an approaching expected stranger; or for a last heartbeat.

Item, One Empty House

EVEN when afternoon tea is unlikely—and, though I had only met my hostess twice or thrice before, I felt pretty sure I should not find her among cups and saucers—it is almost impossible for an English visitor not to arrive about teatime. I was about to do so. It was a foggy January afternoon, and though I kept on rubbing peepholes in the Pullman window and peering out for my first impressions of Connecticut, these did not get beyond the admission that a coating of weathered snow seen in a disadvantageous light looks like a coating of mutton fat and that the contours under the mutton fat were not so rugged as I expected. But no doubt they would soon begin to be rugged. A few nights earlier I had sat next to a man of letters at a dinner party—a dinner party of such magnificence that we drank claret (for all this was taking place in the era of prohibition)—and, learning that he was a Bostonian, had said to him, "Tell me about New England. I am going to spend a night there." Sparing to be particular, since my outlook was so patently general, he told me that New England was reverting to the wild; that the farming population had moved westward and snakes were beginning to come down from the mountains. "Rattlesnakes," said I, knowingly. Looking kindly at me through his pince-nez, the cleanest I have ever seen astride a mortal nose, he said that rattlesnakes were among them, though I should not meet any at this time of year since rattlesnakes hate getting cold; and that he was glad I had read *Elsie Venner*. I told him I had also read about New England in the stories of Mary Wilkins. He replied with an Indeed; and reinforced the effect of withdrawal by adding that she wasn't thought much of now.

Dusk fell on the mutton fat. The contours continued to be calm. Still, here I was in my English tweed suit, getting out at a station in unknown Connecticut as isolated as any pioneer and instantly and astonishingly being recognized by a perfect stranger and driven off in a car along roads where a sledge would have seemed more natural. At this point my memory wavers. But what came next was a large room, full of people, none of whom was wearing a tweed suit and all of whom were talking, and where several kind persons noticed I wasn't drinking and offered me whiskey.

Before I left London I promised various loving friends that during my trip I would on no account drink spirits and go blind (the sequel was considered inevitably part of the deed); and for a couple of days in New York City I was faithful to my vow. Then a loving American friend explained that I mustn't go on like this, since to refuse spirits was tantamount to casting aspersions on one's host's bootlegger—a most uncivil thing to do. As I always listen to the friend that's nearest, I took the plunge and drank whatever was offered me: spirits in ordinary homes, wine in grand ones, and once —so overwhelmingly grand was the home, and able to employ fleets of bootleggers—beer. My eyesight was none the worse for it, and my moral fiber must have been enormously strengthened because of drinking so much whiskey. I loathe whiskey; the only way I could deal with it was to toss it down neat and think of the poor large men in temperance hostels who hadn't got any.

The party in Connecticut was one of those artistic parties drawn from some international Land of Cockayne. I began to slink into corners, to examine the pictures (views of Cockayne), even to wish I could find some reposeful bore. There was nothing to remind me I was exploring Connecticut. I might as well have been in California with those rowdy forty-niners. Finally the outside guests drove away, and the house party began to go to bed. My spirits rose: I had been looking forward to my bedroom. It was in the L of the house, with five tall windows distributed among its outer walls. My hostess came in to ask if I needed anything and to read me one or two of her poems. When she had gone I waited a little longer in case someone else should come in with a few woodcuts or a trilogy. But no one else wanted my opinion; I was left in possession of my handsome bedroom, and went from one window to the next, drawing back the curtains. Outside there were trees. When I switched off the light, the room was flooded with the piercing moonlight of snow and the pattern of branches lay on the floor, so that I seemed to be stepping through a net. Till then I had not rightly felt I was in Connecticut. Now, because of the austerity of the moonlight and the pattern of elm branches on the wooden floor, I did. And I began to think about Mary Wilkins and to reflect that perhaps at that moment I was the only person in New England to be doing so.

I had known her for some time.

After I had been taught to read I was left to read on unassisted. If a title looked promising I tried the book (and thus for years and years never opened Gogol's *Dead Souls*, being convinced it was a work of piety). One day I pulled out a volume called *A New England Nun*. There were two convents in our town, and a nun was a regular feature at the fishmonger's—but nuns in fiction led more animated lives; though my notions about New England were of the vaguest kind and Mary E. Wilkins not a compelling name, the title, I thought, warranted a try. There was no word of a nun; but from the moment when Louisa Ellis tied on a green apron and went out with a little blue crockery bowl to pick some currants for her tea I lost all wish for nuns and animated lives. I had found something nearer the bone. Though I could not have defined what I had found, I knew it was what I wanted. It was something I had already found in nature and in certain teapots—something akin to the precision with which the green ruff fits the white strawberry blossom, or to the airy spacing of a Worcester sprig. But, scampering between balderdash and masterpiece, I had not so far noticed it could happen in writing too.

Having found it, this mysterious charm, I read on how Louisa, after she had finished her tea and washed up the tea things, took off her green apron, disclosing a pink-and-white apron beneath it, which was her sewing apron. This in turn she took off when she heard a man's steps coming up the walk. Beneath the pink-and-white apron was her company apron, of white linen. The man came into the room; he was her suitor, and his entrance, as usual, frightened the canary. He was honest and good and had wooed her faithfully, but in the upshot she dismissed him and remained alone among the currant bushes; and that was the end of the story.

She must have been about contemporary with Maupassant, I thought: the Maupassant of New England, telling her spinster stories as he told his bachelor ones... But one cannot ramble about in a strange house at three in the morning, not even in a bohemian house—indeed, particularly not in a bohemian house—looking for a Dictionary of American Biography and saying through bedroom doors to persons rousing within, "It's all right, it's only me. I don't suppose you happen to remember what year Mary Wilkins was born?"

Besides, it would be a waste of breath. She wasn't thought much of now.

The spinster and the bachelor...He would have thought her a quaint character and put her into one of his stories. She would have surmised him to be a bad character and kept him out of any story of hers. For she had the defect of her thrifty virtues: She wrote within her means, which is why one feels a sameness in her stories —a sameness of effort. Keeping within her means, she chose characters who would not lead her into extravagance, situations that remain within the limits of the foreseeable, never essaying the grandeur of the inevitable. But her control of detail gives these stay-at-home stories a riveting authenticity. The details have the flatness of items in an inventory. Item, one green-handled knife. Item, one strip of matting, worn. They don't express, or symbolize; they exist by being there; they have position, not magnitude. And their infallible, irrefutable placing had fastened so many north-facing rooms, hemlocks, oil lamps, meetinghouses, pork barrels, burial grounds, new tin pails, icicles, and dusty roads into my mind that if I had had the courage of my convictions downstairs, when everyone was talking about Joyce and Pound and melting pots, I would have said, "Why don't you think more of Mary Wilkins?"

I didn't. Perhaps this was as well. For one thing, one should not draw attention to oneself. For another, there might have been someone present who had thought enough about Mary Wilkins to cross-examine my admiration. And then I should have been forced to admit that she couldn't get to grips with a man unless he was old, eccentric, a solitary, henpecked, psychologically aproned in some way or other; that she never hazarded herself; that she was a poor love hand; that lettuce juice too often flowed through the veins of her characters instead of blood. Though in one respect I would have fought hard for her carnality: she wrote admirably about food, about hunger, privation, starvation even. There was that story— which, alas, I did not completely remember because I had read it in a spare room and not had the presence of mind to steal the book— about starving on a wintry mountainside . . .

That bedroom was in Cambridge, England. The biscuit box had gingerbread nuts in it; the presence of my host's top hat in its leather hermitage made me feel I was one of the family; there must have been at least a thousand books on the shelves that occupied one wall—books of the utmost miscellaneity (I had taken Mary Wilkins from between a Bohn Tacitus and *Marvels of Pond Life*); there was a magnifying glass, a bottle of ink, and a bootjack; and at intervals I heard chiming bells conversing in amiable voices about the passage of time. But as I was now in Connecticut and did not wish to grow uncivilly homesick, the best thing I could do was to fall asleep.

When I woke it was broad day. I dressed and went downstairs, reflecting that if I was late for breakfast, this was not an establishment where it would be held against me. It was not I who was late. There was no sound of life, there were no intimations of breakfast. Perhaps this was a house where breakfast was unlikely. In the large room that had been so noisy the night before there were plates and tumblers and bottles and ashtrays; but the curtains had been drawn back, so someone must be about. After a while a young woman came in. She was small and swarthy, and obviously I was a surprise to her. At first she pretended not to see me, and when I said, "Good morning," she clattered her trayful of glasses and did not hear me. I said I was down too early, and realized that she found me difficult to understand, for, smiling anxiously, she waved her hand toward the window and said, "Nice!" and then burst into a speech I couldn't understand at all. But we communicated in the language of the heart, for, beckoning me through the swing door, she took me into the kitchen, where we drank coffee and ate some leftover canapés.

The sun had come out, so I decided I would go for a walk. I followed the road through some woods and on into a landscape of lifeless snow-covered fields. I knew I was not enjoying myself and had decided to turn back when I caught sight of a house about a quarter of a mile farther on. A house standing alone calls to the imagination. I walked on. However trite it might be—and it looked trite—it was a house I had not seen before and would never see again. I began to walk slower—because if you change pace when you come close to a dwelling the people inside will think that you are prying or canvassing. As I approached, I felt certain the house was empty. It was smaller than I thought—a frame house of two stories, lean and high-shouldered, standing a little back from the roadside. It had an air of obstinately asserting its verticality against the indifferent, snow-covered horizontality all around. A fence guarded its own small portion of snow.

I drew level with it, and saw how very empty it was and how forsaken. The gray paint was scaling off it, streaks of damp ran down from its guttering, the windows were bleared with dust and their glass tarnished. They were too large for the house, and this emphasized the disproportion of the door, which was too narrow. A single trail of footprints led from the gate to the door. They were recent, but not new. They might have been made a week ago, three weeks ago. A week ago or three weeks ago someone had gone into the house and not come out again. I stood for a while registering this in my memory—so well that I can see it to this day. Then I turned back, walking briskly because I had grown cold. I did not speculate at all. This was no business of mine. I had come on a story by Mary Wilkins—a story she did not finish.

Four Figures in a Room.
A Distant Figure

THEY had sat down to rest.

Both women were tall and physically eloquent. They appeared to have been engaged in an exploit that taxed them to the uttermost, and they laid by their violin bows as though they were rapiers.

The six-year-old boy lying under the grand piano drawing an alligator glanced out, saw that Fanny's small red velvet bolster lay on her lap unharmed, and went on drawing. All was well. "I can't play without it," she had explained to him. Sometimes—not very often and only if his hands were clean—he was allowed to stroke it. Enabled by the bolster, Fanny played such difficult music at concerts that people gave her a great deal of money. Ludovica also played and also got money but hadn't a bolster.

They began to talk.

"But what are we to do about him? Wouldn't he even listen when you'd gone all that way to see him?"

"He listened—as if he were listening to Clementi. He even patted my hand and said, 'Dear child.' I might as well have talked to the waves. They come much closer to the house than they used to."

"But you could do nothing with him?"

"Fanny! How long is it since anyone could do anything with Father?"

"You did, once—when you got the better of him about the cello."

"And that was forty-three years ago."

"Almost to the day. He had given you a larger one for your birthday present; it had been unpacked and lay on the sofa. Your twelfth candle had just been lit. You took the cake in both hands and banged it down on the bridge."

By the time Donald Gillespie had hoisted himself up in the world and owned the Bonnie Charlie Marine Stores it was too late for him to study the violin. His daughter Fanny was put to do so in his stead—a promising pupil. It followed his second daughter should learn the cello. Ludovica learned quickly, was inherently more musical than her sister; and studied with contempt. Fanny's violin bewitched her; she would have nothing but the violin. Life had not prepared Donald Gillespie to be worsted. He fell into a granite rage and went for a voyage round the world. Pride compelled him to have them well taught even while he taunted himself with rearing a circus act, the fiddling Gillespie Sisters. They made their début together in an unaccompanied Duo Concertante by Spohr. Constructed from their aquiline noses to their sturdy insteps to the ideal specifications for concert violinists, their vocation was plain.

Prompted by the story of the birthday cake, the boy under the grand piano gave the alligator chocolate and pistachio stripes.

"But what does he do with himself on that pocket island?"

"It's not really an island, you know, except at high tide. And he does a great many things and all to a regular timetable. He's got a weathervane and a rain gauge and several barometers and keeps a weather diary. Twice a week he bakes. Every day he goes out and gathers driftwood. He washes and irons and keeps the house like a new pin. He knits. He sings."

"Sings?"

"'Ye banks and braes.' He catches fish and snares rabbits and dresses their skins and reads *Paradise Lost*. Never an idle moment."

"Does he see anyone?"

"The oil van comes out once a week with letters and groceries."

"Does he look older?"

"A great deal older."

The room was warm and smelled of chrysanthemums, and from the street, far below, the growl of traffic swelled up into their silence. Alligators live in swamps. But he had used up all the best greens. This should be a sea alligator, sitting on an island like the very old man they talked about—for as he was their father he must be very old indeed.

Ludovica took up a sheet of manuscript music and made a face at it. "I don't know how he thinks I'm going to get a mute on in the time. You'll have to hang on to your harmonic."

"He has no notion how to write for strings. But one must be grateful for small mercies; there's not much written for two violins nowadays. One has to keep up. And he's got some ideas. We can do something with it—if he'll let us."

"He seemed a meek enough little MacRabbit when Klaus introduced him."

"Meek? With that dedication? 'For Fanny and Ludovica.' Our Christian names and not so much as a by-your-leave."

"The young are like that. No surnames. No key signatures."

"No manners. How much longer is he going to keep us waiting?"

"Well, while he does, let's get on with Father. We can't leave him there through another winter. There must be some way of persuading him."

"Do you know any way to persuade a limpet off a rock? That's what he was like, Fanny. A limpet."

"Limpets must come off occasionally. When we were children we used to pick up their shells."

"Dead."

"What's a limpet?" asked the boy.

They took up their instruments and went back to the opening, which was tricky. Without ceasing to play, Fanny said, "One has to admit it, he's brave."

Julius Morley stepped out of the elevator into a world of his own music. The Dialogue for Two Violins was proceeding, and this was the first time he had heard it. He was overwhelmed by its beauty, its fitness; appalled by its fleetingness. Performance did that, then?—made actual and dismissed? He had not thought of it so. It had seemed boundless, a totality. But it would be over before its hearers had time to admire it. Occasionally passages disconcerted him; it was as if they had got in by accident from an earlier composition. And then it was beautiful again, infallibly logical, going its mysterious way.

Suppose I were run over on my way back to Hammersmith, he thought. I might never hear it again. He unboxed the tape recorder he had brought with him and began to record. Immediately, all his pleasure went; he could hear nothing except the defects of the performance. He rang the bell. The music ceased. The door was opened by a small boy, and he went in.

His heart did not sink; he felled it. They were impossible—professional circus horses, pillars of the Establishment. They advanced on him, capability personified, and were delighted to see him. They thought his music so original. They hoped he wouldn't mind if they made one or two small suggestions, just for technical reasons, reasons of performance. How could he have imagined these worldly harpies matched to his music, administrators of his treasure— cooked them up into his destined Fanny and Ludovica, fatally dedicated the Dialogue to them? A spring evening, an empty stomach, the skirl of gulls as he crossed the river to the Festival Hall, the grieving-seabird fifths falling through the close of the Overture to *Idomeneo*, two women distanced on a platform—two porpoises in bags could have overthrown him that night, playing the Bach Concerto.

"This scale passage would come out with more effect if it were divided between the two violins, for instance, and—"

"Shall we deal with them as we come to them?" he said.

From his lair under the piano (it had become a lair) the boy watched the clock. If his Miss Belton got back in time to take him down to the restaurant for tea— But she had gone on a bus to visit her mother, who lived in Greenwich; she might be late. The minute might have arrived.

They had been playing this piece over and over; he knew quite well when the minute was coming. First they grunted, loudly and mournfully, one contradicting the other. Then Ludovica was left grunting alone, while Fanny squirmed up—and up—and up, and arched her eyebrows, and produced an unearthly squeal like a sweetened gimlet, and Ludovica said, "Blast his eyes!" and snatched her mute. And then it would have arrived: his throat would stiffen, ice would form on his skin, he would begin to cry.

This afternoon it seemed that the bus from Greenwich was

bound to win. Their MacRabbit man did nothing but interrupt and disagree and say they had not understood. And then they played the bit over again, loudly and neatly, and asked if that was what he wanted; and he said it wasn't. Their voices grew crosser and haughtier, and his grew quieter; and if it had not been for what lay ahead if Miss Belton did not come in time, it would have been fun to watch Fanny and Ludovica having to do what they were told. Checked and goaded, the music was driven on. They had got to the growls, Fanny had squirmed upward, attained her squeal—

"Excuse me. No *rallentando*."

They argued and argued. Then Fanny went over to the enemy.

"Get it on somehow, Ludovica! We can't stay fooling about till midnight."

The squeal hung on the air, brightened like a soap bubble, thinned, turned downward like a sigh, and was gone. Beneath it the muted voice had set out on its ghostly wandering. He felt his throat stiffen, ice form on his skin. It was the voice of something eternally lonely and destitute and blind. It probed his flesh. Tears streamed down his face as he wept for joy.

It was because of this coda with its swaying five-beat ground bass that Julius Morley had at one time thought of calling the work *Full Fathom Five*. The Ludovica one did not play too badly, and the mute obscured her professional alacrity. He waited uneasily for the entrance of the unmuted Fanny, who had to slide in on an offbeat (slide, not collide) and thread her shifting tonalities through the ground bass. He scarcely noticed how she did it, for a moment earlier he had been transfixed by a conviction that another listener had come into the room. Covertly glancing round for another pair of legs he saw the boy under the piano and that his face was rigid with ecstasy and glittering with tears. "Another of us," he said proudly to himself. "Poor brat!" The unmuted violin began to take its farewells of the ground bass, which after the seventh farewell would go on its way alone, *senza diminuendo*, till it stopped, insignificantly, like a clock.

The fifth farewell vibrated with emotion.

"Excuse me—"

They ignored him and went on to the end.

"You were going to say—"

Ignoring them, he got up and walked across to the piano. The boy saw him stoop, almost as though he meant to get under, too.

"Do you like it?" His voice was serious; at first sight he looked just as a Mr. MacRabbit should—snub-nosed, with furry cheeks and an innocent expression. On closer view, his face was savage and anxious, as all grown-up faces are.

QWERTYUIOP

The days draw out, the days draw in
(Chop-cherry, chop-cherry, black within),
When will my endless night begin?

URSULA put down her hairbrush and stared at her face in the glass. It was a plump, smooth face, with nothing remarkable about it except a resolute chin. Its reflection assured her that she had made another poem—the first in five days, just when she was beginning to despair. She took the block of lined paper, wrote it down, and considered it. It was one of her best—sarcastic and passionate. But did it say everything as emphatically as it should? Should there be a thump? She wrote it down again and changed the last line.

O God, when will my endless night begin?

With the impetus of a postscript, another poem, cynical this time, darted into her head:

I gave up God when I was nine
(Gooseberry, gooseberry, gooseberry wine)
But put my trust in his name to weigh down a line.

This took a little longer. Finally she copied the one and the other in the careful printing hand she kept for poetry, added the date, and put them in the casket-shaped box that had once held expensive chocolates. She finished dressing and went downstairs to confront her twelfth birthday.

December 31st was a hopeless day to be born on—ten days before she went back to school, ten days before she had anything worth attending to. It was dregs; no one would give her a typewriter so soon after Christmas. There was nothing much to be said for St. Sylvester, either, whose day it was. She had looked him up in the Calendar of Saints in the school library. He was a pope, he tried to establish a general peace, he was venerated at Pisa. She intended to go to Pisa, but it was Shelley she would go for, not poor old Sylvester.

Father was in the hall, putting on his raincoat. He gave her a kiss, and said, "Many happy returns, my pet. I must be off." The door slammed behind him. Mother and Uncle Terence were sitting at the breakfast table, killing time with toast. A bulging parcel in Ursula's place held the woolen jersey Mother had been knitting and hiding for weeks, and a coral bracelet. Uncle Terence handed her a shop-tied oblong. Inside was a manicure set. Mother flushed. Uncle Terence gave her a look and grinned. He was her brother, old enough to be her father, and lived with them as a paying guest. Among her school friends Ursula referred to him as P. G. Pig.

Presently Mother got up and began to collect the dirty china.

Ursula also got up. Sooner or later on this ghastly day she would have to make her bed. But Mother intercepted her, saying, "Come and help me wash up."

She stood at the sink, rinsing and re-rinsing a coffee cup, biting her lips and arranging her expression. When she spoke, it was in her holy voice. "Darling, there's something I must tell you about—"

"Yes, I know. Judy Hollins has got hers already."

The coffee cup slid under the suds. After a pause, Mother began to laugh. "So I've put a packet in your underclothes drawer. Funny sort of birthday present."

Escaping to her bedroom, Ursula sat on the rumpled bed. Life was like that. An hour ago, the four walls had enclosed a kingdom, hers by right and unassailable. Now they gaped on shabbiness and familiarity, and they were papered with those interminable old pink rosebuds. There would be more pink rosebuds on her birthday cake. Year after year Mother had decorated them with pink sugar rosebuds. Sometimes they were quite successful, at other times smudged. She looked at the alarm clock—another of Uncle Terence's hateful presents. She had forgotten to wind it. But the whole house was an alarm clock. There was Mother, drudging with the Hoover; there was Uncle Terence, turning off the radio at the beginning of the Morning Service. How was she to get through this interminable dreary day—drearier now, because it had begun to rain.

There was a knock on the door, and a voice saying, "Am I disturbing you, Miss Ursula?"

"It's Arkie, my darling Arkie!" Ursula leaped up and flung herself into a damp embrace.

"I had to look in on you, Miss Ursula, to wish you your happy returns. So I caught the early bus—"

"Oh, Arkie, you must have got up at dawn!"

"—happen a bit earlier—so as to have a sight of you before I go on to the lady I work for now. There's a poodle dog there, too— pedigree—but not to compare with old Dragon. Stand back, love, and let me have a look at you."

Ursula stood back, remembering not to stoop.

"To think you're a year older this very day. You'll be a lady in no time. But don't study too hard, ducks, lying awake all night with your book-reading. Take life easy while you have the chance."

"Darling Arkie, you've saved my life. It was being such a horrible birthday till you walked in."

"Bound to be even come odd, love—like kippers. I've brought you a little remembrance."

They sat side by side, snuffing the uncorked lavender water and recalling Dragon's exploits, while Mrs. Arkenthwaite's professional eye traveled over the room. Before she left, she made the bed. Byron, too, had his old charwoman, who was faithful to him when everyone else deserted him. It was clear to Ursula that when she went to Pisa Arkenthwaite must accompany her.

At lunch, after the falling pound, Arkenthwaite was the subject of conversation. "The house was so clean we might have been living in the depth of the country instead of Manchester. Terence, do you remember her pork cheese? And Ursula, do you remember the holy- stone patterns she used to make on the kitchen floor? Professor James said they went back to the ancient Britons. Why did she go? I don't know what made her."

"I do. She couldn't stand the way Uncle Terence left his bath tow- els lying about for her to pick up."

"A family trait," said Uncle Terence. "But at least mine aren't filthy."

"More apple pudding, either of you?"

Uncle Terence shook his head, so Ursula ate a second helping as slowly and ostentatiously as she could, folded her napkin with exactitude, and left the room with dignity. Halfway upstairs she remembered that the knitted jersey, the bracelet, and the manicure set were still lying unclaimed. Poor Mother had enough to put up with without her feelings being wounded by an apparent ingratitude for all that knitting: the jersey and the bracelet must be collected, the manicure set conspicuously ignored. She descended. Leaving the room with dignity, she had omitted to shut the door. Their voices were raised. One could not call it eavesdropping.

"The adjective was justified."

"I'm not talking about bath towels. I'm talking about the way you nag at the child. You never miss a chance to say something unpleasant, and then you grin at me as if I were your accomplice. Of course she notices. You mean her to notice. She's sensitive."

"So am I."

"Pooh!"

Mother swept out of the room, holding the tray, and collided with Ursula. Inflamed with chivalry, Ursula picked up two broken pudding plates and some cutlery, and said leave the washing-up to her.

When she had washed everything in sight, paying particular attention to the tines of the forks, and exhausted two dishcloths, and polished the glasses, and swilled the sink and the draining board, she turned round. Mother was sitting sprawled on a kitchen chair, seeming entirely absorbed in breathing. "Angel," she said absently, and went on breathing. Ursula saw herself singlehandedly dealing with heart failure—where were the smelling salts, or did one burn feathers, and where were the nearest feathers?—when Mother drew a sharp breath, sat up, combed her fingers through her hair, and said, "I've been thinking."

"Oh, good!"

"Yes, I've been thinking. What you and I both need is to get out of the house and have a dash of luxury. So I invite you to a birthday tea at the Vienna Tea Room. I'll ring up a taxi at quarter to four."

The Vienna Tea Room was dusky, spacious, unresonant; it was what a church, if thickly carpeted and draftproof, might be, and never was. If Mother hadn't been sitting opposite, though she was actually making no demands, it would have been possible to compose a quite different sort of poetry—less outright, not sarcastic at all:

> On a little gilded chair
> Sit subterraneanly and drink sweet Lethe

In blank verse, probably.

"What about a meringue? Or another slice of *Sacher Torte*? Grand Viennese families had a *Sacher Torte* delivered every day."

"How did you know?"

"That sort of thing sticks in one's head. Now it will stick in yours."

> ... *and drink sweet Lethe* ...

"You must have had a rather different life when you were young."

"I always had Terence. I hated him as a child as much as you do now. Poor Terence! He's always had something wrong with him, something vexing him—migraine, stomach ulcers. Did you know he was married? She was charming, and then went off with another man while he was having an operation. When he came out of hospital, no Susie."

"Is that why we're stuck with him?"

"The odd thing is, your father really likes him."

When they left, the rain had stopped. The wet streets shone between the dark, clifflike housefronts. The traffic speeded, skidded, bellowed like angry beasts. It felt dangerous, not like Manchester. I shall never be the same again, Ursula thought. I shall never be able to call myself my own again. I shall never go to Pisa, never write another poem, never have a typewriter, never see a poem in print. I only wanted the typewriter because magazines think poems in handwriting are by children. I let myself feel interested in Mother, I almost felt interested in Uncle Terence; now I'm trapped. I shall always have to go on feeling interested in them, sorry for them, wound up with them. She heard her feet, step for step with her mother's feet, on the wet pavement.

She had almost decided to be a nun, when her mother stopped. Ursula stopped with her. Mother was hailing a taxi.

"I've just realized how late it is. Your father will be back at any moment, and there's dinner to get."

The change to the unhuman speed of a taxi changed Ursula's outlook. An earlier poet, a Mrs. Greville, had written a "Prayer for Indifference." It was in the school library, and had a lot of verses; when she was back she would look it up and read it more carefully. For indifference was what mattered, indifference was the answer; not to be upset or caught out or involved or understood—above all, not to be horribly, pawingly, understood. Praying was nonsense, of course. No truly indifferent person would pray; he wouldn't need to. His indifference would have insulated him against being sensitive, being annoyed, being interrupted. It would set one above all the daily idiocies—above or apart. Probably apart; keeping oneself to oneself, mysteriously aloof, quellingly calm and polite. Vowed to indifference, Ursula enjoyed the superior sensation of being in a taxi, and was calm and polite when they were caught in a traffic jam and Mother began to fuss about time and dinner.

"At last!" Mother said as the taxi approached the house.

"If we had gone on walking, it would have taken longer."

The taxi drew up. Father also had come by taxi. It was driving away and he was mounting the doorsteps, holding something at the length of his arm. They went in together.

"Here's your birthday present, young lady. Don't drop it. It's heavy." He retrieved it from her grasp and laid it on the hall table. Even before she guessed, she knew. She watched him unclasp the case, lift it out.

QWERTYUIOP

"Oh! Oh!" The second "Oh" was a yelp.

Embarrassed by the sight of her face, smitten expressionless by ecstasy, he began to explain as though he were in guilt and must exculpate himself. "You ought to have had it this morning, but it wasn't ready when I went to collect it yesterday evening. It's secondhand, you see, and I told them to give it a thorough going-over to make sure it was in working order. There's a spare ribbon in the case, and a book of directions, and a brush for cleaning the keys. And paper and carbons. Everything. After dinner I'll show you how it works—which knobs do what. And tomorrow you can start away. Tap-tap-tap!"

He raised his voice. It would be better if Terence did not hear her being so emotional. "You'll find it useful later on, too. There's always work for a typist, especially if she can spell and punctuate.

Not so many can nowadays. Even if you don't learn shorthand and take an office job, there'll always be stuff you can do at home—typing people's novels and poems and so forth. It's my belief that every third person in Manchester is some kind of author. We're a positive nest of singing birds."

He was bound to talk like that, she thought, being a parent. She knew better.

A Brief Ownership

THE Automobile Association had given us a route to Cape Wrath and I was checking it with the Gazetteer of Scotland. "DRUMOCHTER PASS," I read. "The main Inverness road accompanied by the railway traverses this lofty and desolate pass in the Grampians." I saw no harm in that. On winter nights the Inverness road might like to be companioned; and if the car broke down we could wait for the next train. At that point there was a crash in the kitchen and I went off to tell the cat that all was discovered. When I got back, a breeze from the window had flapped over the page. "DULL," I read, "*see* WEEM."

Entangled in an idle curiosity, I began turning over the alphabetical pages of the Gazetteer in pursuit of Weem. In fact, I had not the smallest wish to learn about Weem. We were going to Cape Wrath, and in spirit I had already struck root in Dull.

Dull—as I seemed to know as if I had actually been there—was a small unvisited town in East Fife. It was not even decayed. It was just small and always had been. There was a good ironmonger opposite the War Memorial (the War Memorial was a non-denominational obelisk of shiny granite, to suit all tastes), and a goodish grocer in East Street. Fish came in a van, for Dull was only seven miles from the coast. Dried fish, though, could be got at the greengrocer's, and sometimes cockles, and in July gooseberries, and potatoes and turnips and tinned pineapple at all times of year. From Dull you could go to Cupar. A proverb expressing the philosophy of a race indoctrinated with Calvinism says, "He who will to Cupar maun to Cupar." It is a proverb often on my lips. Even when my hearers don't understand it, they take the stern sense of it and are quietened.

I had settled, however, a couple of miles outside the town. In spring (spring took its time in Dull) the words "DULL LODGE" appeared—loomed, rather—in snowdrops on the bank beside the drive gate. Snowdrops multiply in course of time, and the "g" had got quite out of control. Dull Lodge was a stone-built, slate-roofed, three-storied house, of modest proportions but giving an incontrovertible impression of uprightness. It stood back from the road, and a belt of mixed beech trees and conifers sheltered it from the east wind and the morning sun. From the bathroom window (the bathroom was on the third floor) you could see the melancholy shine of the North Sea. The surrounding country was flattish. There was a pervading smell of sea in the air, mingled with a smell of turnips. Dull Lodge was built in 1850 by a retired wine merchant who had somehow got away from Cupar. It was as plain and purposeful as a ledger, but made one concession to Scottish Baronial in the shape of a small bartizan at the northeast corner. The large sash windows had been put in by the hand of a master. They were totally draftproof, and there was not a rattle among them. Indeed, on stormy nights it could be quite eerie to sit in this impregnable stillness; but comfortable.

The windows were no trouble to keep clean because I had a gardener. He was dumb and went with the place. He lived a quiet bachelor life in a flat over the disused stables, and when his figs and his wall pears began to ripen he tied them up in small muslin bags. As I did no gardening myself, he thought quite well of me.

I did no gardening, because I had gone to Dull Lodge in order to retire. I had furnished it with retirement in view. For once in my life, I had a sufficiency of bookshelves. I also had four black horsehair sofas, which I had bought at a local sale—a couple in the sitting room, one in my bedroom, one in the kitchen. (It is a fallacy to suppose that a kitchen is a fountain of perpetual youth and that the moment one sets foot in it energy courses through one's veins.)

There, on one or another of these admirable sofas, I put my feet up and pursued my researches into the religious life. Research fortifies retirement, which even in a house like Dull Lodge is an imperiled structure, since we are none of us wholly free from conscience: you suppress it about visiting old Miss Tomkins who would be lost without that weekly little cheerful chat on the wickedness of her relations and it starts up afresh in a compulsion to do something for Punch-and-Judy men. But with a good solid blameless piece of research in hand, conscience can howl without and good works blandish like harlots: you are safe, you are buttressed, you may disregard them and continue to lie on your horsehair sofa with your feet up and read about nineteenth-century Church of England bishops.

I had chosen these particular bishops because, except by their biographers, they are singularly unexplored. The light that plays on the *grandes vedettes*, Newman and Pusey and "Satan" Montgomery, leaves them twilit. Yet there they were. I thought a *catalogue raisonné* would not come amiss. At first sight they appear much of a muchness (and undeniably it is a muchness; if I had realized what a lot of them I was taking on, I might have turned to some other subject for research—unicorns, for instance). However diversely they may have begun, whatever vagaries they may have pursued at the university, whatever persuasions may have led them to scratch each other's eyes out, their destiny is their destiny, and by the time they are middle-aged it is pretty clear what will become of them: each in his turn will be ordained bishop by other bishops and merge into the mitered flock. But as a good shepherd knows each of his sheep by something personal to it—a squint, a scar, a pinker nose, a more flippant gait, a more searching expression, a tendency to bloat, a pertinacity in baaing—I hoped to become so conversant with my bishops that I should end by perfectly knowing them apart. Naturally, I had my favorites. I felt a particular affection, positively amounting to approbation, for Bishop Thirlwall of St. David's, who kept cats. Naturally, too, I developed preferences; I preferred Broad bishops to High ones. But High, Broad, or Low, I tried to keep an open mind about them, reading with sympathy of their unmitered domestic hours: the deaths of their wives, the disappointingness of their children, their palace chimneys smoking in a north wind.

And from time to time I found them making remarks of such acumen and humanity that one would have expected everybody to be quite charmed and to leave off snarling immediately, as the animals did when Orpheus played on his lute. Though in fact it proved otherwise.

Thus, moving from bishop to bishop, returning them to the London Library and unpacking new ones (it was extremely rare for a bishop to be unavailable), listening to the wind, watching the changing color of the fields, admiring the snowdrops, eating quantities of ripe figs, tapping the barometer, strolling out in the wistful autumnal dusk when the gardener would not be about to suspect my intentions and even staying out long enough to see the public lighting of Dull extinguished at 10:30 P.M., I lived in contentment and self-satisfaction at Dull Lodge.

And then I turned over another page of the Gazetteer and had seen "WEEM." In a flash I was out of Dull Lodge, away from the horizon of sea and the gulls and the good ironmonger and a far cry from Cupar.

"WEEM," I read. "Perth. Early closing Wed. Lies on the north bank of the River Tay. 2½ miles W. is the hamlet of Dull, preserving an old Cross, while in the vicinity are various prehistoric cairns, standing stones and remains of stone circles."

No.

No, such a Dull wouldn't do. The Tay is a noble river and we shall cross it with admiration on our way to accompany the railway to Inverness. Preserving old Crosses is a laudable industry. Prehistoric remains are pleasing to the young. In short, the revealed Dull, 2½ miles E. of Weem, was in every way a superior article. But it wouldn't do. It wasn't what I had in mind. And the moral of all this is, as usual, Leave Well Alone. By grasping at the substance, I have forfeited the lovely shadow. By fidgeting through the Gazetteer in pursuit of Weem—a place of no interest to me except as an adjunct to Dull (so peculiarly my own)—I have lost Dull Lodge, I no longer possess a property in East Fife, I am not even retired.

In the Absence of Mrs. Bullen

WHAT had began as a lick and a promise, provoked by Mrs. Bullen's telephone call ("Sorry, Miss, but I shan't be able to come today, nor the next few days, actually. My sister-in-law's been took worse, and while I'm about it, I expect I'll stay for the funeral..."), had hardened into a thorough turnout of the sitting room; such a thorough turnout that Leonora had broken off to dress the part, assuming one of Mrs. Bullen's overalls, tying up her head in a duster, and changing into an old pair of sandals. Mrs. Bullen worked on spike heels, but Leonora had been taught in her youth what is sense and what isn't. To be properly armed for the fray is half the battle—a maxim, like keeping your powder dry and not buying fish on a Monday. Those spike heels might well be accountable for the dust along the skirting and the cobwebs that clothed the back of the radiator. An element of scorn for Mrs. Bullen's halfhearted purifications heightened Leonora's zeal, and sharpened her self-satisfaction as though it were the vinegar trickled into the mayonnaise. But she did not allow herself to be swept away; she imagined no rebuking conversations to take place when Mrs. Bullen came back from her sister-in-law's funeral. Charwomen were nonexistent in Pew Green. Mrs. Bullen was a Londoner, and traveled to and fro on the Metropolitan, and you don't lightly shake the faithfulness of someone ready to do that for love of your art.

Fifteen years before, when Leonora told other lovers of her art that she had bought a cottage in the peace and quiet of the country, and that when she had added a garage with a proper bathroom over it and replaced rhubarb and cabbages with moss roses and lavender, it would be her dream cottage come true, Pew Green was still a village on the outskirts of London, with its own pretty little slum of real cottages with working-class families in them. Postwar housing developments had changed all that; embedded among natty bungalows that were born with garages and bathrooms and had gardens foaming with floribundas, the vestigial Pew Green looked faintly comic, looked, in fact, very much what Leonora in moments of depression was afraid of becoming herself—a leftover. But she stayed on, from inertia, from prudence, thinking that when the day came when she could no longer sing for her living she would be able to sell the freehold of Bramble Cottage as a building lot and do quite well out of it. Just now that day seemed a long way off. Stimulated by virtue and housewifery, she felt as lively as a flea. Her voice, a durable contralto, was as good as ever, her genre as much in demand—more so, indeed, since she had had the foresight to build up a new repertory of songs with religious appeal, to match the new feeling for religion; and her appearance, though inevitably bulkier and bulgier, was just right for the television career of a sweet-faced motherly woman singing welcomes to prodigal sons and cajoleries to St. Peter. All this she had jeopardized a few years before by giving way to an impulse to make a feature of "Ta-Ra-Ra-Boom-de-Ay." This revival of a beefier past hadn't done at all, and like a person of sense she had dropped it. Yet while it lasted it had been a releasing rapture.

Ta-ra-ra-boom-de-aying sofa cushions was being quite releasing, too, and further satisfactions awaited her: the bowl of detergent suds into which she would plunge her Staffordshire poodles, the polishing she would give to her silver ornaments, the lager chilling in the refrigerator, the slices of underdone cold beef she would eat in her fingers, the digestive repose with her feet higher than her head. It was quarter past eleven on the longest day of the year. On the longest day, every hour is as good as a day in itself; there would be hour after well-spent hour before she need get into her black and go off to Rusty's party to meet that guitar-playing fellow who might have a song for her.

At eleven-twenty someone came whistling to the door and rang the bell. Since the interruption whistled, it must be something being delivered—flowers, perhaps. She could do with some nice tributary flowers. The supply wasn't what it had been since old Mr. Jameson had gone to dodge death duties in the Isle of Man. Odd, really, when you had no one depending on you, to take such a high moral line about death duties. The whistle broke off as she opened the door. The whistler was a young man with a little bag—one of the new young men, with a coiffure and an intellectual expression.

"Morning. Is this where Miss Leonora Keeling lives?"

After all, why *should* he have recognized her? Looking a damned sight more motherly than she cared to think, and sweat-faced into the bargain, she could thank her stars that he hadn't recognized her. But she didn't want him coming in. "Miss Keeling is not at home."

Instead of going away, he stood there smiling at her. "I've come to do the piano. I'm the new tuner."

"Miss Keeling will be out all day."

"Tut-tut! Never mind, I don't suppose she'd want to overhear every note of it."

"And I'm in the middle of turning out the room."

"That won't worry me. I can work through anything. Just get me a clean duster and I'll be no more trouble to you. Which way do I go?"

Leonora had sometimes imagined herself saying, "Leave my house this instant!" The hour and the man had never combined to make this possible. They didn't now. She saw him take off his coat, open his bag, and begin to rip the piano to bits in the usual ruthless way—only in this case it seemed more markedly ruthless.

"Somewhat dusty, is it not?" He hoo-hooed into its interior, and a wiry sigh responded. "Off we go!"

Tum. Tum-tum.

While she stood in the kitchen, boiling with frustration and choosing out a quellingly flawless duster, it suddenly occurred to her that she had seen no tuning fork. Suppose he was one of those take-in thieves, only waiting for her reappearance to gag and bind the poor old charwoman and make off with her mistress's jewelry? He was steadfastly tum-tumming, still making unsatisfied bites at that middle A—but this might be only a blind. One can tum-tum with one hand while the other tightens its hold on a weapon. She took the duster that came uppermost, and hurried back.

"Here you are. Why, where's that thing you do it with—what's it called? Tuning fork. Haven't you got one?"

"There's one in the bag. But I don't use it. I don't need to. I've got absolute pitch."

It was clear that jewels would mean nothing to him, nor wine, women, revenge, the call of the wild, the Archbishop of Canterbury, the Isles of Greece. He had absolute pitch.

"Don't let me put you off whatever you were doing in here. It won't worry me."

"Speak for yourself," she muttered, and slammed out of the room. Tum. Tum-tum.

The sound pursued her. It possessed the house, as if it were some indifferent occupying power, a foe from the moon. She went back to the kitchen—there is always something to do in a kitchen—and began to count those dusters. Tum-tum. She lost count, left them, polished a spoon, saw a smeared wineglass, and rubbed it. The stem snapped under her energy. Tum-tum. She took herself into the garden, and began weeding. The sound was in the garden, too. Her occupation withered in her hands. She returned indoors, and on an impulse flushed the toilet. The noise of her defiance subsided. Tum-tum. Tum-tum. On other piano-tuning occasions, she had always gone out, with a blithe "Offer him a drink, Mrs. Bullen, if I'm not back in time." For a moment there was silence. Then he began his probing again. Tum-tum-tum, farther up the keyboard. "I shall go mad!" she exclaimed. "Damn Mrs. Bullen!" For that matter, she could go out now, flouting him with the roar of the accelerator, leaving him and his absolute pitch to get on with it by themselves. Tum. Tum-tum. But the thought withered, as the expedient of weeding had done. It was impossible to decide on anything with that noise in the house—impossible to think, impossible to act, impossible to exist except as the attendant on those disembodied fidgetings, enforced, just when she was getting used to tum and tum, by an interposition of chords, or a chromatic scale, or an iteration of gaunt fifths. Tum. Tum. Now he had gone back to the middle of the keyboard, just about where he had started from. Good God, could nothing satisfy him? Why couldn't he leave well enough alone, as other people did? Besides, what was this perfection he was tum-tumming after? That chilblained Miss Varley, with all those letters after her name like mixed biscuits—L.R.A.M., F.R.C.O.—what was it she used to bore on about? Intonation, intervals, some major thirds being more major than other major thirds—the gist of it was that in order to seem in tune whatever the key you played in, half the notes on the keyboard had to be out of tune. A properly tuned piano was, like everything else, a fake. A fake, a fake! Tum. Tum-tum. That was all he was achieving.

"No better than the rest of us," she exclaimed. "I wonder if he knows it?"

He was now right up at the top of the keyboard, making a noise like a dripping tap. All that fuss about a note you wouldn't want to play more than once in a twelvemonth.

The doorbell rang. Careless as to whether she would again be mistaken for her charwoman, she hurried to answer it. It might be someone who would come in and talk. It was the man to read the electricity meter, who recognized her instantly and remarked, "You've got the piano tuner in, I see." She kept him as long as she could, but he was not a man of much conversation.

She was resigning herself to more solitary endurance, now of being knelled at—for the piano tuner had shifted his attentions and was probing the abyss—when she realized that a silence had become longer than other silences had been. Into it broke a coruscation of arpeggios rushing from end to end of the keyboard. It was over; he was playing the voluntary. He must be offered refreshment. She could do with a whiskey herself. She carried in a tray with cigarettes and glasses and the decanter, only to learn that he neither smoked nor drank.

"But if I can have a glass of milk—"

"Modern, aren't you?" she said, availing herself of the freedom of being Mrs. Bullen. Availing herself of the freedom of being Leonora Keeling, she poured out a double whiskey and tossed it off. Flown with milk and principles, he would not notice any discrepancy between the two freedoms.

He didn't. "Tell Miss Keeling that I have put in some moth crystals. It's an old instrument, but that's no reason why it shouldn't be looked after." He closed the piano, he closed his bag. "I daresay she values it for sentimental reasons." He handed her the duster. "That's one of the things I like about Miss Keeling. She doesn't try to be modern. She's content to sing those quiet, old-fashioned songs. I think a woman should be her age—she is, anyhow, so why try to conceal it?"

"Have some more milk."

"Well, thank you . . . I'd really be glad of it."

Returning with more milk, she found him gazing out of the window.

"Moss roses, aren't they?"

"I'm sure I can't say. Some sort of roses."

"Moss roses. It's a curious thing, but I always connect Miss Keeling with moss roses."

"Why? She hasn't got whiskers."

He wrinkled his pure high forehead in a frown of rebuke. "Miss Keeling is an artist I think very highly of. I have a complete set of her recordings. I should think that's unique. I may say that the earlier ones took a lot of finding. I had to advertise in the *Exchange and Mart*."

"What's it you think so specially highly of?"

"Her sincerity. I feel she's so sincere. The first time I saw her on television, I said to myself, 'This is a good woman, who's been tried in the furnace and come out of it as sweet as an old-fashioned rose.' So naturally, when I saw those moss roses in the garden, I was quite struck. I'm like that, though. I can always tell a person's real character. I daresay it's something to do with my absolute pitch."

"Do you like her voice?"

"I always like a contralto. It's my favorite voice. And she puts so much feeling into hers. That song 'Little Irish Donkey'—the way she sings that last verse! 'Close your patient eyes, for when you've climbed the last blue hill you'll be in paradise . . . '" It was flatteringly obvious that he had listened most attentively.

"Is that the one you like best?" she asked, the performer's insatiable lust to have everything liked best rising in her. "What about 'Now You Are Home'?"

"Yes, that's certainly one of my favorites." As though he had learned it at her knee, he welcomed the prodigal. He also Loved His Autumn Roses Best of All, thought of His Neighbors' Sorrows too, and meditated on the Old Sewing Machine that was Silent Now. He had quite a good voice, warm and caressing, and plenty of it. She was dreamily wondering whether she oughtn't to take to milk when she saw him putting on his coat.

Should she tell him? It would give him the thrill of his life, and one doesn't meet such an admirer every day. Should she ask him to stay for lunch?

"Well, I must be going. Remember to tell her about the moth crystals. I wish I could have told her myself. To tell the truth, she's always been a sort of mother image to me. Well, I'll be back next quarter—perhaps I'll meet her then."

"If you do, I'm afraid she'll be a bit of a disappointment to you."

"Disappointment? Why? Is she—isn't she as strong as she was? Now I come to think of it, she hasn't been on the screen lately."

"She's as strong as she was, all right. You should see her going round and round this room doing the high kicks and singing 'Ta-Ra-Ra-Boom-de-Ay.'"

"Ta-Ra . . . ?"

"Song you've never heard of, young man. Goes like this."

The first couple of kicks dislodged the sandals; the next loosened the duster; a specially ardent kick wrenched the buttons off the overall and split her skirt to above the knee. Round and round she went, singing louder and louder, kicking higher and higher, growing more and more giddy, and each time that she neared him she saw the young man take another cautious backward step toward the door. When she lost her balance and fell, he made no attempt to pick her up.

Squirming into a sitting posture, she wriggled herself round to face him. Gathering her breath together, composing her features, she assumed her public-appearance expression, smiled her sweet-faced motherly smile, freed her jaws:

"Little Irish Donkey," she intoned.

"It's disgraceful, disgraceful! You're not worthy to work for such a good woman. I don't believe a word of it!"

But as he rushed out of the room, it was plain that he believed more than he supposed.

Still on the floor, sitting bruised and breathless amid the scene of her thorough turnout, Leonora contemplated her extraordinary behavior. What a way to treat a piano tuner! What a way to treat one of her public!

"Couldn't have acted otherwise," she pronounced with solemnity. "No one with the soul of an artist could have acted otherwise."

For though it was news to her that she had the soul of an artist, she accepted the revelation. It isn't what you do that matters; everyone has a right to earn a living, and fooling a willing public is as good a way as any other. They enjoy it, you enjoy it, everyone's happy. Where the soul of an artist comes in is when you won't let the public fool you. Owing to an unfortunate train of circumstances that began when she tied up her head in a duster, she had almost yielded to the sweetness of being fooled. But not quite. The soul of an artist had seen to that. She was saved. So was the beef. If she had asked him to lunch, she would have had to give him all the beef. There was not enough for two.

Afterword

by Michael Steinman

To read these twenty stories by Sylvia Townsend Warner is to delight in a world of wit, anarchy, and sometimes mournful splendor. Most were published in *The New Yorker* but none were reprinted in collections, perhaps because she preferred writing stories to putting together books. They are satiric, fantastic yet clear-eyed, and populated with lively characters: a child-poet, two violinists, a nymph, Lord Byron. These characters find themselves amid equally lively things and events: a mean-spirited saucepan of milk, a heel-kicking rendition of "Ta-Ra-Ra-Boom-de-Ay," a breakneck funeral service, an invented Haydn quartet. Neither characters nor settings are predictable, yet at the close of a Warner story everything we have encountered seems inevitable.

This collection begins with houses and their inhabitants, both observed with equal care, for Warner respected the powers that houses, estates, and beautiful things can hold over those who fancy themselves their owners. Although suspicious of wealth and authority, she created tender romance out of the reunion of a beloved object and its rightful owner in "A Flying Start" and "The

Listening Woman." Yet one person's ownership is another's deprivation, making her stories of Mr. Edom's antique business inescapably political. The same can be said of the title story.

In "The Music at Long Verney" (1971) we make ourselves comfortable in a milieu only to be suddenly turned out of it. Of the origin of this story, Warner told William Maxwell: "I saw this couple standing outside their own house and had to know how they got there." Given its opening sentences, which depict the ancestral mansion as a burden, readers might foresee social comedy about traditions upended; given that Warner was seventy-six when she wrote the story, readers might also expect her to praise mature wisdom, to satirize the callow young. True, the young couple's wealth comes from an herbicide that kills nightingales, and they illuminate their evening musicale with church candles, but Warner does not idealize her elderly Basil and Sybil even as she solicits concern for them. "Improbable and dreamlike," the story records warfare between landed and exiled, between classes and generations, but it celebrates no victors.

"The Inside-Out" (1972) also depicts exile and removal, dramas enacted by children unhampered by polite behavior. Warner finds the strange in the prosaic—the unpainted backs of furniture, a weedy garden containing a leaf-filled bathtub. The story asks us, "How can we know the boundaries of the prison? Which of us is the interloper? How should we greet the savages?" I think Warner's pleasure in not answering is tangible. "Flora" (1977), the last story she published in *The New Yorker*, uses a supremely banal object, a white plastic garbage pail, to reveal a great deal about a man, boorish both as host and as scholar. "Maternal Devotion" (1947) depicts the Finch family, the circus-act of "The House with the Lilacs" and other stories of the forties, in a suitably unbalanced environment. Here, Cordelia Finch tosses an unwanted suitor to her mother, whose conversational talents exhaust him even as they delight us. With her limitless enthusiasms and unpredictable associations, Mrs. Finch is Warner's "only essay at a self-portrait; her conversation and her ineffability. A limited and very laudatory self-portrait, but the resemblance is there."

David Garnett told Warner, "What you write best about is love." "An Aging Head" (1963) considers two varieties of the phenomenon —the choking affections of relatives and perverse romantic couplings. It is a Warner rocket, the short story as "sniping." (As she once told a friend, "You can pick odd enemies off, you know, by aiming a short story well.") Aunt Georgina seems another self-portrait; Warner, active well into her seventies, resented condescending solicitude. "Love" (1972), more affectionate, echoes "The Music at Long Verney": it too has two couples, youthful and mature, and a house in transition, yet this time Warner's praise of marital devotion is wholly without irony. At its close, a husband muses on the sleeping wife he reveres but knows incompletely—they are a happier pair than those other troubled sleepers, Gabriel and Gretta Conroy.

"'Stay, Corydon, Thou Swain'" (1929), its title taken from John Wilbye's madrigal, improvises on classical metamorphoses. Perhaps a man who joins a woman named Cave to bicycle through a mysterious wood lacks necessary caution? Warner's compositional gifts are wonderful here; she stops the story abruptly where a foolhardy author would have gone on. "Afternoon in Summer" (1972) follows a pair of ardent contemporary lovers, generously including murder, cannibalism, starvation, a funeral, and a headstone in its bucolic way. All will be well: mortality is held at bay, Time is killed, Sally and Willie feast on each other. "A Scent of Roses" (1972) is less benign; the sky *is* falling. As in Warner's classic story "A Love Match," ardor and war intertwine.

Named for a beloved artifact whose mystery deepens, "Tebic" (1958) sweetly celebrates marriage; as a study of the proper giving and receiving of presents, the love both acts embody, it is peerless. Tebic itself, at once adorable and Sphinxlike, explains much about the stories of Mr. Edom, his assistant Collins, buyers and sellers, objects and ownership. "Real and dear" to Warner, the antiques dealer takes his name from Genesis, although Warner forgave her Edom for putting his birthright on sale. The stories showcase the same gift for mimicry that got her "dismissed" from kindergarten as "a very bad influence." An antique shop was made for such comedy; as she wrote Maxwell, "All professions in this country seem to have highish proportions of maniacs and eccentrics, antique dealers eminently so. In a quiet way, too; which makes them even more striking."

"A Flying Start" (1963) observes a husband and wife whose tastes in beautiful objects differ. When his desires override hers, she acts for herself, silently applauded by Mr. Edom. "English Mosaic" (1964) is animated by a sublime example of Warner's visual slapstick: a drainpipe decorated with rare porcelain smashed into recognizable bits, an offense that Mr. Edom takes personally. In contrast to "English Mosaic," "The Candles" (1966) is elegiac. A portrait of an electrical blackout, it offers an inspired meditation on the power of candlelight to evoke lovely, lost time. A complacent writer might have said that the scene became "mysteriously beautiful and enriched"; Warner's revery is poignant, strange, and fleeting. "Furnivall's Hoopoe" (1970) fills the shop with outlandish people, among them an unprincipled ornithologist devoted to the "post-mortem preservation" of British birds (another Warner rocket) who battles with other patrons for an ungainly piece of Victoriana. "The Listening Woman," the last Edom story, was written in 1965 but was not published until 1972, as William Shawn, editor of *The New Yorker*, had wearied of the series. The painting described here had been in Warner's family from her childhood and now hangs in the Dorset County Museum. Although comic misreadings proliferate, the story is mournful, even when separated lovers are reunited.

The concluding group of stories depicts artists at work, including Warner herself, and the power of the imagination to create or distort, a recurring subject throughout her work. In "Item, One Empty House" (1966), Warner's recollections of a guest house in Connecticut turn into an imagined story—unwritten and unfinished—by Mary E. Wilkins Freeman. It is as if she had seen objects from her window and had construed them in her own way. "Four Figures in a Room. A Distant Figure" (1973) asks "Who owns music: the performers, the composer, the listener?" Warner had studied composition and practice and was an expert on Tudor church music. But her questions about interpretation echo her relations to those who tried to impose their own structures on what she had written. (Explaining the little boy under the piano, she wrote, "I am a realist and constantly facing the unexplained," which points a helpful way in to her world.) Stories of suffering writers are often self-indulgent, but Warner transcends this in "QWERTYUIOP" (1977). Her poet, Ursula, despairing and inspired, is constrained by childhood, although her longings, her anger, and her Romanticism are fully adult. "A Brief Ownership" (1967) improvises on place names, freeing Warner to invent a contented life filled with horsehair sofas, Anglican bishops, Orpheus, and ripe figs. So sure was her invention that *The New Yorker*'s fact-checking machinery stuttered and lurched, certain she was describing a real town. The final story, "In the Absence of Mrs. Bullen" (1962), is a virtuosic display in which an